A SOLDIER'S FOREVER

BEYOND VALOR 2

LYNNE ST. JAMES

A Soldier's Forever

Copyright © 2018 by Lynne St. James
Cover Art Copyright © 2018 by Lynne St. James
Cover Art by LoriJacksonDesign.com
Published by Coffee Bean Press
Created in the United States

This book is a work of fiction. Names, characters, places, and incidents are products of the author's imagination or used fictitiously. Any resemblance to actual events or locales or persons living, or dead is entirely coincidental.

No part of this work may be used, stored, reproduced or transmitted without written permission from the publisher except for brief quotations for review purposes as permitted by law.

This book is licensed for your personal enjoyment only and may not be re-sold or given away to other people. If you would like to share this book, please purchase an additional copy for each person.

If you're reading this book and did not purchase it, or it was not purchased for your use only, please purchase your own copy. Thank you for respecting the hard work of this author.

❀ Created with Vellum

A SOLDIER'S FOREVER

Chloe loves Logan with all her heart but when she learns she's pregnant with their third child and about to spend their tenth anniversary alone it's not exactly the celebration she'd hoped to have. But as a military spouse with her husband on a deployment she'd make the best of it.

Between dust storms and unseen enemies, Logan has been reconsidering his life choices. When he's offered an opportunity to go stateside for an assignment, he jumps at the chance. With the help of his best friend, Alex, he plans a romantic weekend on Sanibel Island.

When Logan surprises Chloe with a romantic

trip it's like a dream come true. But instead of being able to enjoy their time together, she's worried about his reaction when he finds out she's pregnant. Being the primary parent while he's in constant danger thousands of miles away is getting old. But will he be willing to give up his military career for his family?

Between seashells and sunsets, will their love be able to ride out the storm to find their forever?

DEDICATION

For all the spouses and families who are the cheerleaders, support systems, and anchors for our military!

As always, for T.S., you're the inspiration for all my heroes. I love you!

NOTE TO READERS

This book was originally titled *A Soldier's Surprise* and published as part of the Barefoot Bay Kindle World. If you already own the original story, it is not necessary to purchase this version. However, it has been re-edited, and a substantial amount of new content has been added.

CHAPTER 1

"Mommmm!"
Oh God, what now? Chloe wondered as the shrill screech echoed through the house. What did Lexie do this time? "Okay sweetie, finish getting dressed. I need to check on your sister." Chloe waited for her five-year-old daughter Bella to nod.

"Lexie's in trouble," Bella said with entirely too much glee.

"That's not nice."

"She's always in trouble." That was too true. Ugh. What were the odds Lexie had spilled the gallon of milk again? Or maybe, the Eggo waffle was burning and she couldn't 'Leggo her Eggo.' Gotta love mornings. Not.

As she stepped into the kitchen, the problem

was instantly obvious. "Crap. Lexie, shut off the water."

"I tried, Mom. It won't stop." Tears slid down her daughter's face, leaving shiny trails of frustration on her flushed cheeks.

"It's okay, honey. I'll get it." Reaching for the faucet, Chloe turned the cold water knob, but instead of shutting off the water, it came loose and fell into the palm of her hand. She cursed under her breath as the water shot straight up like a geyser and drenched them both.

"I wanna play in the fountain," Bella said from the kitchen doorway.

"No. You need to stay where you are. You just got dressed."

"But Mommy..."

"No buts."

"Yeah, Bella. Listen to Mom," Lexie echoed. Chloe rolled her eyes at 'her little mini-me' as she knelt on the floor and reached under the sink for the shut-off. The valve wouldn't budge. Why did everything go wrong when Logan wasn't there? Stupid question since he was hardly ever home. Putting all her weight behind it, she tried again without success. Water poured over the edge of the counter like a waterfall and drenched everything.

Wrestling with a stubborn valve had not been on her agenda this morning and the last thing she needed. As the water rained down on her, she struggled to stay upright as her knees slid on the slippery tile. Ending up on her butt in the middle of the rising lake that was her kitchen floor looked more and more likely as she continued to struggle with the ornery valve.

As Bella and Lexie argued back and forth, her frustration level rose with the sound of their voices. Just about ready to give up, shut off the main water supply, and call a plumber, she decided to give it one last try. Focusing all her strength on her metal nemesis, she prayed it would give in to her superiority. Seriously, enough was enough. Then it moved, at first only a hair, but then she pushed with everything she had, and it turned. She almost cheered when her silent prayers were answered. No more rain. Thank God. Then the honking horn from her driveway reminded her how far behind they were and cut short her celebration.

"C'mon girls, cut it out right now. Lexie, go upstairs and get changed. Aunt Lily's here to take you to school."

"Why aren't you taking us? I don't want to go with Aunt Lily. She always wears her PJs."

Not one to miss an opportunity, Bella chimed in. "Me either."

Counting to ten, she gave Lexie the dreaded "mom" look. Every kid knew the look and complied or knew there'd be hell to pay later. "Go. Now. It's not up for discussion. If you don't hurry, you're going to be late for school."

"What about lunch?"

"I'll give you money. Bonus, right?"

Bella cheered and Chloe rolled her eyes. She could see it now, they'd be eating French fries and ice cream sandwiches. One day wouldn't hurt much, she hoped and added making their lunches before she went to bed to her mental to-do list. Last night they'd Facetimed with Logan and she'd forgotten all about it. It was the constant exhaustion, and it had been getting worse. After falling asleep at the dinner table, she gave in to her inner mom voice and made a doctor's appointment. It wasn't normal for her to be so drained all the time. Maybe life was catching up to her. She wasn't as young as she used to be. None of them were, all she had to do was look at the girls. They had grown like weeds. But this felt more like old-fashioned burnout. A vacation to recharge was out of the question. She was lucky to have a few hours of downtime while they were in school. Even that wasn't going to last much longer. The school year was almost over.

It was ridiculous how fast time flew by and every year it was worse. It was hard to believe she and Logan had been together for almost thirteen years, and that their tenth anniversary was in two days. Ten anniversaries and Logan had only been home for three of them. This year would be no different. Such was the life of a military spouse. At least they had Facetime. It had been worse when he'd first deployed when they were dating and had just gotten married. Phone calls had been few and far between then.

Chloe pulled the mop out of the pantry just as she heard the back door open. Knowing it was Lily, she turned to see her come to an abrupt halt. As Lexie predicted, she was wearing her PJs. Today's selection was penguins with matching fuzzy slippers. She wasn't surprised, as Lexie said, it was her typical attire.

They'd met during high school and been best friends for almost twenty years—more than half of their lives and were closer than most sisters. Lily's idiosyncrasies didn't bother her, she had more than enough of her own quirks to balance it out. All that mattered was that they could count on each other no matter what, and it had been that way since the beginning. Lily's ability to make her laugh was just a bonus as far as she was concerned. But seeing the horror then amazement flash across Lily's face made her giggle. It didn't matter that she was soaked from head to toe or that her hair dripped water down her face, her expression was priceless, and she knew what was coming next. Chloe counted to five, it was only a matter of time. Wait for it. Wait for it.

"What the fuck happened here?" Yup, there it was.

"Oooh. Aunt Lily, you said a really bad word. You have to put money in the curse jar." Chloe almost choked at the look of accusation on Bella's face. Go figure. For once the child listened and hadn't moved from the edge of the kitchen.

"Well shit. Sorry, munchkin. I'll get right on it." Fat chance. If Lily put money in the jar every time she 'used a bad word' she'd have been able to book a trip to Hawaii for the entire family.

"Bella, go see if your sister is dressed yet." After a moment's hesitation, she ran down the hall and clunked up the steps yelling for Lexie.

"So again, I ask, what the fuck happened? Were you playing mermaid or something? Shame on you, you know it's a school day." Lily said as her eyebrows disappeared under her sandy-brown bangs.

Chloe shrugged. "Honestly, I'm not sure. I was more concerned with getting the water to stop. I think somehow the faucet broke when Lexie was rinsing her breakfast dish. Guess it's another thing to add to the 'honey-do' list."

Lily rolled her eyes and Chloe almost laughed again. Adding to the list had become an almost a daily occurrence since Logan had left after Christmas. "No shit."

"Aunt Lily!" This time, both girls nabbed her.

"Damn."

Their looks were priceless, which made Lily's sour expression even funnier. "Give Aunt Lily a break. She had to get up early to take you to school. Now she's waiting around for us."

"Are you ready?" Lily asked as she backed out the door.

"Mommy, you didn't give us lunch money," Lexie reminded her.

"Shit, sorry."

"Mommy…"

"I know, Bella." Chloe took a quarter out of her wallet and gave it to Bella for the curse jar. Then she tucked five dollar bills into each of their backpacks as she hugged them. "Give me a kiss. I'll see you after school. Don't forget you have gymnastics later, Lexie."

"I won't."

"Bye, mommy."

"Love you, girls. Be good today."

"I'll be back with some Starbucks. I think you need it," Lily yelled over her shoulder as she led the girls outside. Who would turn down Starbucks? Not in this life. She hadn't even had her first cup of coffee yet.

Grabbing the mop, she finished cleaning the floor while relishing the quiet. A scarce commodity in their house. She loved the girls but had to admit the constant arguing got old. Or maybe it was her patience that was wearing thin. The peace and quiet wouldn't last for long. Lily would be back in about fifteen minutes, and she still had to finish wiping down the counters and shower before her doctor's appointment. Her alone time melted faster than ice cream on a hot summer's day.

Melting ice cream reminded her of their first real date. Who brought ice cream on a picnic in July in Florida? Logan had been so cute. He'd planned the entire date as a surprise. She was lucky he told her to wear something casual. After picking her up, they'd driven to the beach. Then he'd pulled out a huge basket from the back seat of the car.

It looked like something out of a Hallmark movie, especially when he pulled out the red checked blanket and spread it out for them to sit on. Wine, fried chicken, potato salad, and then the puddle of ice cream for dessert. He was mortified, but it was one of the main reasons she'd fallen for him. Maybe when he came home next time they'd be able to get some grown-up alone time. Since he'd been home at Christmas she probably had to wait until the end of his deployment and that wasn't for six months. Just thinking about her husband put a smile on her face. She loved him with every fiber of her being and hearing his voice still sent shivers down her spine. Not bad after ten years.

Chiding herself for daydreaming when there was so much to be done, Chloe finishing cleaning up 'Lake Mitchell' and then used her phone to search for a plumber. She was still looking when Lily came in balancing two coffees and a bag of something that would probably make her gain weight.

"What time is your appointment?" Lily asked as she sat at the kitchen table.

"Ten," Chloe answered as she inhaled the scent of freshly brewed coffee.

"When do we need to leave? Oh, I Googled it, and I bet you're anemic. I mean we're not getting any younger and you have two kids. It's typical for women, especially your age. It's either that or mono," Lily said, as she batted her eyes. Yeah right, mono at her age and from kissing who?

"I don't know. I don't have a fever, but I'm always exhausted lately. There are times it's a struggle to keep my eyes open right after I wake up."

"Why didn't you tell me you weren't feeling right?"

"Because I'm just tired. Besides when do I ever tell you when I'm sick?"

"True. But it's bad enough that your kids even noticed. Lexie said you've been, and I quote, "falling asleep all the time and really cranky." The two of them discussed it all the way to school. Bella thinks you need a teddy bear to sleep with while her daddy is away, so you aren't sad."

"Poor kid. Lexie is growing up too fast, and Bella, she's just Bella."

"Yup, definitely my goddaughter." Chloe agreed. Bella couldn't have been more like Lily if she'd been her child.

"Did you call a plumber yet?" Lily asked as she pulled a croissant out of the paper bag. Chloe's mouth watered. The buttery deliciousness would go right to her hips.

"Nope. Surprising I know. But it's the one service guy I haven't needed to call. Do you know one?"

"Ha. Of course I do. My piece o'shit has as many issues as yours. Let me call 'Mommy's Little Helper' and see if he can come this afternoon."

"Seriously? That's the name of your plumber?"

"Yeah. I can't believe I haven't told you about him? It was hysterical the first time he came. I had to have told you."

"I don't remember."

"Hmm maybe you've got a brain tumor."

Chloe rolled her eyes. Lily was addicted to WebMD and God help it if you mentioned any kind of symptom.

"I doubt it."

"Maybe. Anyway, I don't know what the fuck I expected but it sure as hell wasn't the Maytag man."

"Maytag man?"

"You know, the guy in the old TV commercials." Chloe couldn't place it, but then she didn't have a television addiction like her friend.

Lily pulled out her phone and clicked on the YouTube icon and in a few swipes, she found an old Maytag commercial. "He could be his twin, I swear."

"Your 'Mommy's Little Helper' looks like that?"

"Yup," Lily said as she burst into a fit of giggles. "Can you believe it? I thought it would be some hot guy showing up, but instead, I got Henry—his real name. I had to struggle not to laugh in his face. Hell, I even put on clothes."

"No way. You got dressed during the day when Alex wasn't home?"

"I know. Can you believe that shit?" Chloe giggled too and soon they were both clutching their stomachs. It happened every time they got together, and it didn't stop until their tummies cramped, and they were gasping for breath.

"Your reputation is going to be ruined."

"No shit. Hey, you'd better go shower, or we're going to be late for your appointment. I'll give Henry a call while you're getting ready."

"Crap. You're right. I'm sitting here like I have all the time in the world. I'll be right down." Chloe wrapped her arms around Lily for a quick hug before she climbed the stairs to take her shower.

∼

"Fucking sandstorms," Lieutenant Logan Mitchell grumbled, mostly to himself as he shook the sand out of every piece of clothing he took off. It was one of the many things about Afghanistan he could have lived without. Every day the list grew a little longer. Halfway through his third tour, he figured he'd earned the right to bitch, at least to Alex. The two men had been friends since college. They'd met in ROTC when they'd signed up after nine-eleven and had been inseparable. Somehow, they'd even managed to be stationed together most of their military careers and now fourteen years later they were in Afghanistan for the third time.

"C'mon, you know getting sand in every fucking orifice is the best thing ever."

"Fuck yeah, of course it is, asshole." They looked like walking sand monsters. Covered from head to toe in beige dust like something out of a horror movie. He'd replaced his sunglasses after the last storm a few weeks ago, and now the new ones were scratched all to hell. Maybe he should buy stock in the company and supplement his income.

"You're just jealous that I don't have sand up *my* ass, princess."

"Do you really want to go there?" Even though Logan didn't want to admit it, Alex was right. His team had been out all day on maneuvers and were on their way back to base when the haboob hit. Less than four clicks from camp when the billowy wall of dust coated them in hot grit. It sucked donkey balls.

"By the way, the captain wants to see you."

Logan cocked an eyebrow. "Did he say why?"

"Nope. Not a word."

"Well, fuck. This day just keeps getting better and better."

"Have you been up to shit I don't know about?"

"How would that be possible? Besides, you're the troublemaker. But c'mon, 'he wants to see me?' That's never good." It had to be a problem, or he'd have caught up with him at mess. "Wanna bet?" Logan asked as he stowed his gear and sat on his bunk to pull off his boots.

"Sure. Fifty bucks."

"Wait. You jumped on that too damn fast. Fifty bucks? And he didn't say a word about why he wanted to see me?"

"Yup. And no, he didn't. I've got one of those feelings."

"Are you sure it's not lunch?" Alex flipped him the bird as Logan went to grab a shower.

There was no 'asap' with the message, and he'd rather not be covered in sand when he saw the captain. The shower took care of most of the grit, but some of it was embedded so it looked like patches of sandpaper. They'd been wearing full gear, but the sand managed to find a way inside of everything anyway.

After the shower, he guzzled two bottles of

water, and even then he couldn't get the dryness out of his throat. It would have to do for now. He had an appointment he needed to get to. It was only twenty minutes later when he saluted the captain in his office. Captain Durant was career military, third generation, and did everything by the book. It could have made things rough, but he was a decent man. Rules were rules, but when it came down to it, he always put the men first.

"At ease, lieutenant."

"Yes, sir."

"Anything to report?"

"No, sir. Just another haboob."

"I'm glad to hear the only issue was a little sand." Easy for him to say, he wasn't caught in it.

"Is there a problem, sir?"

"Not at all. I've got an assignment for you. You'll have to go stateside for a few days."

"Stateside? What's up, sir?

"The colonel needs someone who can explain what we're up against out here. There's a joint task force meeting at MacDill. Word around camp is that your anniversary is coming up. I figured it would kill two birds with one stone. Take care of the briefing and have time with your wife." Alex strikes again. No wonder he wanted to make the bet. He'd been flapping his dick beaters again.

"Thank you, sir. I appreciate the opportunity."

"You won't be thanking me when you have to deal with the colonel at the briefing. But you'll have a few days with your family." The captain handed him a thick envelope. "Your presentation material. The colonel was his usual pompous self, but then, when isn't he? This should have you covered. Basically, you need to tell them what we're up against, be blunt, anything else won't fly. Just tell them like it is, you've been here long enough to know, and it just might put you in front of the right people. I know you've got a review coming up."

"I understand. Thank you, sir. I'll make sure to leave a good impression."

"Of course you will, or I wouldn't be sending you. Get your gear together, the transport leaves at eighteen hundred hours. See you in four days and give my best to Chloe."

"Yes, sir. Thank you, sir." He couldn't wait to let her know he was coming home. Although just showing up would be one hell of a surprise. Logan didn't know whether to shit or go blind.

It took all his years of service to maintain his demeanor until he got out of the captain's office. He had to find Alex and let him know, although he'd bet another fifty he knew all the details already.

CHAPTER 2

"Let me get this straight. You're almost four months pregnant, and you had no idea? How is that even possible?" Chloe couldn't believe it either. How had she missed all the signs? It wasn't her first rodeo. Her periods were always irregular which made it harder to keep track, but she should have realized.

"Yup, apparently. Holy crap. A baby…" Her voice trailed off as the magnitude of the situation hit her. Would Logan be happy about another baby? They'd never talked about it, and after Bella, she pretty much figured they were done. Maybe this one would be a boy. Oh man. She'd have more kids than hands. It was about to get a whole lot more complicated around there.

"You okay?"

"I think so. Wait. Of course, I am. I'm in shock, but totally good. Uh huh. Yup. Oh my God, a baby."

Lily snorted. "No shit? It's just dawning on you? Wait until you're huge and have to pee every ten minutes. We've been down this road. I didn't think we were traveling it again."

Chloe giggled. She hadn't planned on it either. So much for trusting condoms. Surprise. Was she happy, of course, thrilled even, but the prospect of being almost thirty-two and raising another child on her own was a little daunting. "Sorry, brat. Looks like you're in for a third go 'round.'"

Chloe was sorry, too, especially when she caught the wistful gaze Lily tried to hide. She and Alex had been trying for years to have a baby with no luck. They'd been married for eight years but with Alex away so often, it wasn't like she could try infertility treatments. Somehow, Chloe had managed to get pregnant at Christmas when Logan was home. What were the odds? Maybe they should stop on the way home to pick up some lottery tickets.

"It's okay. You know how much I love the whole birth thing. Maybe we'll be lucky, and Logan will be home this time."

Rolling her eyes, she dug her keys out of her purse and opened the door of Lily's car. "Want to come in for a while? I don't have to pick up the kids for a couple of hours."

"I can't. I have a deadline for the ad campaign for *El Tucan*. I told you about it, remember? The new Mexican restaurant that's opening next month. They need the presentation by the end of the week and I'm only about half done. Unless you need me?"

"No, I'm good. Maybe Henry will show up early to fix the sink."

"Don't count on it, but if he does be careful of the crack, it's deep." She snorted at her own joke. "Call or text if you need anything," Lily yelled through her open window as she backed out of the driveway.

Home again, Chloe glanced at the clock on the stove told her she had about two hours before she needed to get the girls from school. A nap sounded good, but there was always something to do, laundry, cleaning, grocery lists. Without thinking, she turned on the Keurig and grabbed her favorite mug. Lily had helped the girls make it for Mother's Day last year. She owed Lily a lot, and once again, today she'd been there when she needed her.

Admitting she was worried would never happen, but it didn't change the fact that she was. She really needed to stop listening to Lily. It had been stupid to worry. If she'd thought about it, she would have known she was pregnant. Even with all the Zumba classes, her pants were tighter than ever, and the scale had been going in the wrong direction. Instead of losing another ten pounds before Logan came home, she'd be gaining a lot more if this pregnancy was anything like her other two. Logan. Damn. How was she going to break the news? On Facetime? It wasn't a discussion she wanted to have over the computer. But face-to-face was pretty much out of the question.

By the time the Keurig was ready she remembered the rule. No coffee during pregnancy. Shit. It was almost the worst part. No coffee for the next five months would be absolute torture. Yes, she'd done it twice before and survived but she was older now, with two kids who wore her out. With a shrug, she grabbed a glass and filled it with water from the fridge. It would be her drink for the rest of the pregnancy and while she breastfed, another six or seven months at least.

A yawn convinced her that a nap was the perfect way to spend the next couple of hours. She grabbed the blanket and curled up on the couch. Yawning again as she put her head on the pillow, she was asleep almost as soon as she closed her eyes.

The loud ringing of her phone alarm dragged her out of her dream and back to reality. Thank God she'd had it set for daily reminders or she'd be late to pick up the girls from school. Disaster averted. As she ran upstairs to brush her teeth and change her t-shirt, she caught a glimpse of herself in the mirror. Damn. She looked like crap. Tangled hair, pale skin, and dark circles. Welcome to pregnancy. It appeared her 'glowing' period was running behind. Brushing out the tangles, she pulled her hair into a ponytail, ran downstairs, and then grabbed a water bottle on her way out the door.

The carpool lane was backed up as usual, but at least she wasn't late. Pulling up to the curb, Bella's teacher opened the passenger door and leaned in as the girls climbed into the back seat.

"Hi, Mrs. Mitchell. Have a great afternoon. Bye, girls. See you tomorrow."

"Thanks, Mrs. Swain, you too."

She closed the door and backed away as Chloe checked the rearview mirror. As she pulled into traffic the afternoon marathon began. Gymnastics for Lexie, ballet for Bella, and then home for dinner and homework. It was exhausting just thinking about it.

~

Not only had Alex known about the assignment, but he'd pulled up a website on his computer to show him the White Sands Resort & Spa. After he'd found out Logan was going home, he and Lily made reservations for them as an anniversary gift. Sneaky bastard. But the most surprising is that Lily knew and hadn't slipped and told Chloe that he was coming home. If everything went according to plan, it should be one helluva surprise.

He'd made it to the transport with a half hour to spare and settled in for the long flight to Germany. After that, it would be another plane home to Florida. It was hard to contain his excitement at seeing his wife and girls again, but he settled down to review all the materials Captain Durant had given him to prepare for the meeting at MacDill. With any luck, he'd get through it before he landed in Florida and would have more time with Chloe. When he focused, the silkiness of her skin and the light scent of jasmine surrounded him as he nuzzled her neck and filled him with desire. Thankfully, no one was sitting close enough to notice the bulge in the front of his fatigues. Squirming in his seat to alleviate the pressure, he grinned and shook his head. Even after all this time she still did it for him. Settling back into reading through the packet, his heart was lighter than it had been since he'd left after Christmas. It had been harder than usual, and he'd longed to stay with his family. But as always, he'd hugged and kissed his three beautiful girls and went back to the desert.

The girls were growing like weeds and he'd missed so much of their lives. Never there to see their accomplishments, the ballet recitals, the gymnastics demos, the school plays, he'd missed them all. He should have stopped the trip down memory lane with the thoughts of Chloe. Now the heaviness returned with the morose thoughts. Shaking it off, he decided he'd spoil Chloe at the resort.

A spa day was the perfect way to pamper his woman. She'd had to deal with so much on her own and stuck with him for the last ten years without one complaint. The woman was a saint. He'd been blessed. Chloe was the woman of his dreams, and Alex was the brother he'd never had, even if he was a total pain in the ass at times. He'd been the closest thing to family he'd had before he met Chloe.

The White Sands Resort & Spa was huge and had just about everything you could want and a price tag to go along with it. Alex and Lily had spent way too much. He'd told him that too. As usual, Alex had responded with a smirk and the standard, "Bro, don't worry you'd make it up to me." He'd never be able to, but knowing how much Chloe would love it, he'd gladly give him anything he wanted.

The only hitch in the whole trip was the meeting at MacDill. The Air Force Base was about a two-hour drive from the resort, and he'd spend most of Monday away from Chloe, but hopefully being spoiled in the spa would make it up to her. If he'd planned it right she'd be just finishing up when he'd be returning from the meeting. Ten years of marriage. He loved her more now than the day he spoke his vows as he stared into her sky-blue eyes. They'd been so young, so naïve, but even with him being gone more than home she'd stuck with him and given him two daughters.

After reviewing the list of spa services, Logan's head was spinning. He had no idea what Chloe would enjoy, but he knew someone who would. Sending an email, he asked Alex to check with Lily to let him know what she'd like. A convoluted way to go about things? Hell yeah. But if it meant she'd have the most pampered day of her life it was worth it.

It didn't take long to an answer and armed with her suggestions, he called to make the spa appointment when he landed in Germany, rather than waiting and risking that they would be booked solid. Now that everything was set for Monday while he was at MacDill, he didn't feel as bad about having to leave her for the day. Then when he got back, they'd have a romantic dinner at the Thistle Lodge, the resort's fancy restaurant on the beach. Perfect.

The flight stretched on for what seemed like forever, and he'd crossed more time zones than he wanted to remember. Frustration sucked at him, patience was never one of his strengths. He hated to wait for anything, and age had done nothing to mellow his disposition. It took all his willpower not to text Chloe and see how she and the girls were doing. It would have sent off flares, and she would have known something was going on. He needed to suck it up—another 'Alex-ism.' Sun glinted on the plane's window and practically blinded him, not that he cared. It means they were on their final approach and Logan watched as the gentle waves of the Atlantic Ocean broke against the sand. He was home. Finally.

It was arranged that Lily would be waiting at Fitzsimmons AFB to drive him home. Being Lily, it was debatable whether or not she'd be on time. Her lack of punctuality was a standing joke with all of them, especially her husband, who reminded her often that she'd be late to her own funeral.

It turned out he didn't have to worry. As he exited the aircraft, she was waiting, and she was in regular clothes. "Holy shit, girl. You didn't have to get dressed up for me," he said, pulling her into a bear hug. Once again, he realized how lucky he and Chloe were to have the Barretts as friends.

"It wasn't for you, jerk. Alex told me the captain didn't appreciate my lack of decorum when I came on base. I wanted to tell him to go take a flying..."

Logan saluted as the colonel approached and was thankful Lily stopped short before she said what he knew was coming next. That's all he would have needed.

"Colonel. Nice to see you, sir."

"Lieutenant Mitchell. Captain Durant said he was sending you as his representative at the meeting. He assured me you'd be able to handle whatever we throw at you."

"Yes, sir. No problem. I'll double check with the captain for any updates before Monday."

"Excellent. Don't enjoy your R&R too much. I expect you to be on time. You know it's at MacDill, correct?"

"Yes, sir."

"Good. I'll see you Monday. Carry on." With a nod at Lily, he continued to the waiting helicopter.

"Damn, woman, that was close. You need to watch your tongue."

"Don't tell Alex, please."

Logan grinned. "No problem, kiddo. I need to check in and make sure everything is set. I'll meet you out front. I want to get out of here before someone else comes along."

"You got it. I can't wait to see the look on Chloe's face when she sees you. She's going to shit a brick."

"I kind of hope she doesn't, I'd rather get a different reaction."

Lily winked at him and walked around to the front of the building to wait for him. Logan was counting down the minutes until he could pull his wife into his arms. It had been almost four months since he'd seen her, but damn if it didn't feel like forever.

Grabbing his paperwork, he ran outside and climbed into the passenger seat of Lily's car. "How's Alex doing?"

"Same as always, I know he misses you. We're both pretty much over Afghanistan at this point. This tour has sucked the life out of us."

"I wish he'd ask to be stationed here. You guys are always gone." Her words echoed what he'd been thinking on the plane. But the fastest way up the chain of command was to be in the field. He still had over ten years before he could think about retiring. The army was all he knew.

"I know it's hard for you. For Chloe too,

especially with the kids." He saw her grimace and realized he'd put his size thirteen foot right in it. Damn. "I'm sorry."

"It's fine. I've kind of given up on the whole idea of kids. Besides with Alex gone all the time..." Her words trailed off as she turned onto their street. As soon as he saw his house his heart sped up and his palms were damp.

"Ready, soldier?"

"Hell yeah." As she pulled the car into the driveway, she blew the horn. Her usual arrival announcement. Then she hopped out and he followed her to the kitchen door.

"Hey guys, I brought a surprise," Lily announced as she opened the door. Lexie asked if it was doughnuts, and he had to stifle his laugh as he stepped through the door. Chloe looked up from doing dishes and when she saw him she dropped the glass she was washing. The sound of glass shattering echoed in the stunned silence.

"Surprise!"

CHAPTER 3

"Logan? How the...?" She stopped herself before the "curse patrol" could jump all over her. The girls charged her husband as he attempted to step into the kitchen. They wrapped their little arms around his waist, and he lifted up to give them kisses. His strength never ceased to amaze her.

"Daddy!"

"How are my little princesses?" Logan kissed them on their foreheads, but his gaze was locked on Chloe.

Heat crawled up her cheeks as she remembered how she looked—hair in a ponytail, dark circles, no makeup. Not exactly how she'd want him to see her after being away. Oh well, that's what no warning got him. Emotions raced through her mind and she tried to pin one down. Stunned. Confused. Elated. She didn't know how he'd managed to be standing in their kitchen, but she wasn't going to complain. Then she caught Lily's knowing smile and realized that's why she'd been avoiding her since yesterday. She'd never have been able to keep the secret otherwise.

A dishtowel was thrust into her hands, which were still in the hot soapy water along with the shattered glass. She blinked and smiled at Lily, as she was elbowed. "Are you just going to stand there? Shit, woman!" Lily was lucky the girls were busy with Logan, or they'd have jumped all over her about her cursing.

Snapping out of her momentary stupor, she dried her hands and tossed the towel on the counter. Then she ran to Logan and stopped just short of jumping into his arms. He hugged the girls then put them down to pull Chloe into the embrace she'd been fantasizing about for the last four months. Their lips met in a scorching kiss, heating her from the inside out. Chloe melted against him as she wrapped her arms around his neck and pressed her body against his solid wall of chest.

They ended their kiss as the girls' "ewws" and "gross" comments finally sank in. As she pulled back she searched his face. He looked exhausted. There were new lines around his eyes and at the corners of his mouth. His temples were peppered with gray hairs that hadn't been there in January. But when she met his sapphire-blue eyes they were burning with desire. Heat rose in her cheeks and dampness flooded her panties with the promise of what was to come.

Gently setting her down, he pulled her against his side and he answered the question she hadn't had a chance to ask. "A special assignment came up. I wasn't going to turn down a chance to see my girls." She missed the sound of his voice, his wide bright white smile, but not being able to touch him or hold him left a gaping hole in her chest. It didn't matter how often he left, whenever he returned it was always as magical as the first time.

The girls jumped up and down in front of him and talked over each other as they tried to get his attention. It was the same every time and would last a couple of hours before the household settled down again. It was okay, she didn't care how crazy his homecomings were as long as he returned to them.

Chloe kissed Logan's neck and whispered, "Welcome home, sexy." His eyes twinkled, and he winked.

"I have an even bigger surprise for you."

"Better than this?"

"Oh yeah." The girls were still chattering, and Chloe didn't want to keep him from them even though she was dying to know about the surprise.

"I'll order some pizza. You can hang out with the girls while they bring you up to speed. It's the only way we'll be able to talk."

"Sounds like a plan. Don't forget the extra pepperoni."

"Like I could," she answered and rolled her eyes. As he tried to swat her butt, she ducked out of reach and laughed. "Lily, do you want to stay for pizza?"

"Daddy, don't spank Mommy. She wasn't bad."

Logan grinned. "Okay, Bella. I won't spank her. As long as she's been good."

"Except for the bad words. But Aunt Lily is worse," Lexie chimed in, nodding her head toward the curse jar on the counter. Of course, she'd have to tattle.

"I think that's my cue to leave. I'll take a raincheck on the pizza. Have fun. Call if you need anything," Lily said as she headed toward the door. She whispered in Logan's ear as she passed him and waved to Chloe as she pulled the door closed behind her. Curious. What had she said to Logan? Before she could ask him, he picked up the girls and carried them off to the family room.

The kitchen had gone from full of life and laughter to empty and quiet. Out of nowhere a feeling of dread slithered down her spine. Shaking it off as being silly, she grabbed the phone and ordered the pizzas. While waiting for the delivery, she cleaned the broken glass and finished washing the dishes and finished as the doorbell rang.

Instead of calling them in to eat, an impromptu welcome home picnic sounded like a much better idea. Juggling the pizza boxes, paper plates, juice boxes for the girls, and a beer for Logan, she concentrated on her steps. It never failed, every pregnancy she'd get the dropsies and she wasn't taking any chances. She smiled just thinking about the little life growing inside her, and with Logan home, things couldn't get much better. Now she just had to figure out how to tell him their family was going to increase by one. Hopefully, he wouldn't notice she wasn't drinking beer since she wasn't quite ready to spill the beans. All she wanted was to be in his arms and make love until they wore themselves out.

∽

The girls didn't stop talking until the pizza came and then only long enough to swallow. Logan had forgotten how wired they were. It had only been four months since he'd last seen them, yet they'd changed so much. The warmth and love that filled his home made life on base feel like he'd been on some desolate planet. And it was all because of Chloe, without her his life would always be a barren desert.

The spouse of a soldier was never easy, as hard as it was for him being off, he admitted she had the harder job of raising their children to be good people. And she'd always done it without complaint. But she looked tired and was quieter than usual, and it worried him. Then again, maybe she just couldn't get a word in between Bella and Lexie's constant chattering.

As if she knew he was thinking about her, their eyes met and a beautiful smile spread across her face. There was his girl. Gorgeous. Damn, he'd missed her. Facetime wasn't cutting it. Or was he just getting old and sentimental? It could be time to rethink his career choices.

"Daddy, did you hear me?" Chagrined at being caught not paying attention by his five-year-old, he pulled Bella into his lap and hugged her.

"Sorry, Peanut. Daddy is tired from the trip. Can you tell me again?" He tried to concentrate, he really did. But exhaustion permeated every fiber of his body. Even lifting the girls was becoming a chore, and he struggled to keep his eyes open. The stress of the last few months had been worse than usual and taken a toll. Enemy combatants grew more and more hostile, and from the briefings they'd received and what they'd seen on the news, it wasn't just in Afghanistan. The world was more dangerous than ever before.

His team had discussed it a lot lately, especially after Mac's unit had taken a direct hit last year and they'd lost four men. Tag lost his arm and leg and Mac almost died. It might not have been their unit, but they were their friends and it had affected all of them. There were many on his team who were thinking of not re-upping at the end of this deployment, and he couldn't say he blamed them. He had eight months left, but a decision would have to be made sooner than later.

The discussion needed to happen, but this weekend was about making up for all the anniversaries he'd missed. To show her how much he loved and cherished her, and that his life wouldn't be worth shit without her and the girls. She'd been his support, his partner, his heart for so long that any changes to their future needed to be made together, but it could wait for now.

"I think Daddy needs a break. He'll still be here tomorrow, and you can talk to him then. It's getting late anyway, time to get ready for bed."

"Do we have to?" Bella whined.

"Yes, you do. It's a school night."

"But Mom, Dad's home. He's never here, can't we stay home from school?" Lexie begged, and Logan winced at the reminder of his constant absence. He was lucky the girls remembered him since he'd been gone most of their lives.

"Nope, you only have a few weeks left before summer vacation. Daddy will be here when you get home tomorrow."

"Yes, I will," Logan answered as they turned to him for confirmation. He wondered if they'd be upset when he took Chloe away for the weekend. He'd already arranged for them to stay at Lily's house and he was sure they'd have a great time. At least, he hoped so.

"Will you tuck us in, Daddy?"

"Of course."

"Read a story too?"

He couldn't hold back his smile. Same old Lexie, always looking for a way to get more time before lights out. Definitely his daughter. "Yup. Pick out a book. I'll be up as soon as I help Mom clean up."

They trudged up the stairs, and Bella muttered under her breath but loudly enough to make sure everyone would know she wasn't happy. Chloe covered her mouth to hide her smile. "Don't forget to brush your teeth. I'm going to make Daddy smell your breath, and he'll tell me."

"We will," Lexie answered over Bella's

grumbling. Lexie acted more like a little adult than a seven-year-old. After seeing how she'd been all evening, he understood what Chloe meant when she said Lexie tried to mother Bella all the time. They'd bickered back and forth at least three times over dinner as they volleyed for his attention. It had to be hard dealing with them on her own.

Chloe grabbed the dishes and glasses, and he followed her into the kitchen with the pizza boxes. Nothing like Genna's New York Style Pizza to satisfy his pepperoni craving. Too bad he couldn't bring some back with him.

"I see what you mean about Lexie."

Chloe smiled. "I didn't think it would take long. It's gotten a lot worse over the last month. I don't know what triggered it, either. I think she's trying to help, but Bella definitely doesn't appreciate it."

"That's obvious. How have you been handling it?"

"I talked with Lexie the other day and it helped for about five minutes. I'm not sure what else to do. I guess they'll work it out or kill each other trying. It's life experience, right?"

"Sounds good to me. As long as they don't start hand to hand combat."

"Well, no shit. Oops. Good thing Bella didn't hear that," Chloe said with a grin. Bella had explained over dinner how Aunt Lily cursed all the time and soon they'd be able to go to Hawaii. It was like listening to a miniature Chloe. Too bad he couldn't take her to Hawaii, but hopefully she'd love White Sands Resort & Spa.

"Should I get the jar for you?"

"Umm, no that's okay." Chloe laughed as she finished putting away the leftover pizza. As she closed the refrigerator door, he grabbed her from behind and pulled her against him. Nuzzling in her hair, he inhaled the aroma of lemon verbena. Her scent. One he'd carry with him through the gates of hell. It had saved him many times, pulling him back from the darkness that hovered around him.

"I missed you, Princess. Damn, you smell so good." Sliding his fingers over her cheek and into her hair, he lifted it away from her neck. As his lips touched the silky skin below her ear, Lexie called from upstairs. Would he ever have a chance to give his wife a proper hello? At his sigh, she lifted her eyes to his.

"It's okay. Go read to them. I'll be up in a minute. Do you want another beer?"

"You read my mind." He only intended to give her a quick kiss, but as their lips touched his desire ignited. He took her mouth the way he wanted to take her, possess her, remind her that she was his. But Bella's yelling broke the spell. "I love you, Chloe. I hope you know how much," he said, his voice rough with emotion.

"I love you too, with all my heart. I'm so glad you're home."

"Me too. I have another surprise too, but you'll have to wait until we get the girls to bed." From the smirk on her face, he figured she thought he meant sex. She was in for a big surprise. He couldn't hide his grin as he turned and headed upstairs to read to his daughters.

CHAPTER 4

A surprise? Sure. He wouldn't be awake long enough to get out of his fatigues. They'd been through this routine so many times. He had the best intentions, but without fail by the time she got into bed, he was out like a light. Exhausted from the trip home, the deployment, stress, all of the above. It didn't bother her—not really. Not that she didn't crave his touch, his taste, how he turned her into a puddle of pure bliss. But snuggling against him meant the world, even if he was out cold and snoring loud enough to shake the walls. This time, she'd probably be fast asleep cuddled up against his warmth. The pregnancy was draining her stamina like she had a slow leak. The prenatal vitamins she was supposed to pick up from the drug store would probably help, if she remembered to get them. Yawning wide enough to make her jaw crack, she giggled. All she had to do was think about sleep and she yawned.

The baby. She needed to tell him. But when? They hadn't even discussed how long he'd be home. All he'd said was that he had a special assignment. Whatever that meant. As much as she'd prefer to tell him in person, but what if he wasn't happy about another baby? Having him home, no matter how long, was a gift. She didn't want anything to ruin it.

The baby was a surprise for her too. It was the last thing she'd expected the doctor to tell her, but it didn't mean she wasn't as thrilled as she was the first two times. But how would he react? He seemed a little overwhelmed by the girls, especially during dinner with their non-stop chatter. It didn't faze her until they started picking on each other until one of them cried, usually Bella.

After another yawn and a quick check to make sure everything was put away, she grabbed a bottle of water and a beer for Logan and headed upstairs. Her first surprise was not finding him asleep in one of the girl's beds.

She'd figured they'd fall asleep while he was reading. When she didn't find him with the girls, she headed down the hall to their bedroom. The light was on and she didn't hear him snoring, maybe they'd have a 'surprise' tonight after all.

Toeing open the bedroom door, she heard the water running in the shower. Steam poured through the open bathroom door and filling their room with a damp haze. She never understood how he didn't scald himself the water was so hot. When she'd asked him about it, he'd said it made up for all the pathetic ones he had to deal with in the desert.

The damp heat took her breath away as she stood in the bathroom doorway. "Hey, dude. How about leaving some hot water for the rest of us?"

"I have a better idea. Why don't you come in? Then you won't have to worry about it."

"I don't think so. My poor skin would never be the same. I know how hot that water is."

"I'll turn it down. C'mon Princess, you know you want to." He was right, she loved showering with him, especially when he washed her hair. There was something so sensual in the way he massaged her scalp and feathered his fingers through her hair. It turned her into a big puddle of mush before he'd even touched any of her erogenous zones.

How could she turn down an offer like that? Without a moment's hesitation, her clothing hit the floor. Naked, wrapped in the damp fog, she reminded him, "You'd better turn it way down, or I'll look like a lobster."

"Already done, Princess," Logan replied in a voice that was pure sex. It sent a shiver of pleasure down her spine. Would he notice her little baby bump? Maybe he'd chalk it up to weight gain, she was an old married woman. According to her mother, women of a certain age all gained weight. Her theory was flawed. Her mom didn't have an extra ounce of weight on her so where she was coming up with that crap Chloe had no idea.

Twenty minutes later there wasn't a drop of hot water left and they were forced out of their steamy cocoon. Wrapping her in a towel, he grabbed a second and dried her hair, then worked his way down her body. Following the path of the towel with a trail of kisses. When they were dry they climbed into bed, and he pulled her against his side. She snuggled closer and rested her hand over his heart.

"I've been afraid to ask, but how long will you be home?"

A huge grin spread across his face and crinkled the corners of his eyes. "That's part of the surprise."

"You mean there really is a surprise?"

"Yup. I know what you were thinking, but you're wrong." He lifted her chin with his finger and slid his tongue across her lips before dipping into her mouth. At his touch, a sizzle of electricity traveled along her nerve endings all the way to her toes. He pulled her onto his chest and the slight dusting of hair tickled her skin. Sighing into his kiss, her breath quickened as desire heated her to her core.

"Damn."

"What?"

"We need to talk, but you feel so good."

"What's wrong?" Hearing those fateful words, her happiness evaporated into worry.

"Nothing's wrong. Shit, I'm doing this all wrong. I had it all planned, and I'm fucking it up."

"Just tell me already." Not letting her go, he wrapped his arms around her as he leaned against the stack of pillows. When their eyes met, she didn't see anything scary so maybe it would be okay, but she needed to hear it from him. Why was he stalling? If he made her wait much longer she was going to her lose her shit.

"I have to go to MacDill to do a briefing Monday."

"Okay, no big deal. It's near Tampa, right? That's only about three hours away. Does that mean we have you until Sunday?"

"Not exactly." Starting to get frustrated, she smacked his chest. He'd said it was a surprise, that was supposed to mean something good. She needed to hold on to that thought, or Jerky McJerkface was going to get worse than a smack.

"Will you just freakin' tell me before I get pissed off?"

"Okay, okay." Mischief danced in his eyes, and she couldn't imagine what he was up to. "I'm taking you with me. Alex and Lily got us a room on Sanibel Island at the White Sands Resort & Spa. We're going to celebrate our anniversary—alone—thanks to them."

"What?" She'd heard him. She really did. But it was like he was speaking a language she didn't understand, or one her brain couldn't process for some reason. She'd been so prepared for bad news that her brain couldn't keep up. "Lily and Alex got us a room at a resort?"

"Alex heard the captain talking about the meeting and how he didn't want to fly back for it. So he suggested I do it. After telling the captain it was our anniversary, he was more than happy to push the trip off on me. It's no secret he and the colonel don't get along."

The confusion began to fade, and the words were making sense again. "Holy crap! A weekend away. Alone with you? Really? Hell, I'd be happy if it was the Holiday Inn down the street."

"Princess, you have no idea. Wait until you see this place, it's freaking amazing."

"When do we leave?"

"Early Saturday morning. We can spend Friday night with the girls doing family stuff, then drop them at Lily's on our way out. It's all arranged. We'll drive to Sanibel Island and then Monday morning I'll head over to Tampa early, but we'll still have Monday night together before we check out on Tuesday morning."

"Oh my God. I'm so excited. I should be mad at Lily, but I can't, it's…oh my God wonderful. I can't even…Wow."

If the smile on Logan's face had been any

wider, his cheeks would have cracked. They hadn't been away since before the girls were born. The excitement filled her with energy and desire. Jumping off the bed, she grabbed a suitcase out of the closet. As she stood contemplating what to pack, she was lifted up and carried back to bed by her sexy man.

"There is plenty of time for packing tomorrow while the girls are in school. I've needed you since before I walked through the door. I can't wait another minute." Logan rolled her onto her back. His scorching kiss made everything evaporate except for the desire tingling along her nerve endings.

His roughened fingers slid over her naked body leaving heat in their wake until she burned brighter than any flame. Their passion for each other had never faded, maybe because they spent so much time apart. When he parted her thighs and his tongue touched her, all thought dissolved in a burst of pleasure.

"Damn, Chloe, I wanted to take it slow. But I can't wait. I'm sorry."

"Don't, no reason. I want you, I need you..." Before she could try to form the words, he was buried deep inside her. Tiny pulses of pleasure bloomed into a full-on explosion and shattered the little bit of control she had left. Moaning his name, she clutched his shoulders and quivered with her release. Seconds later, he groaned as he thrust once more and filled her to overflowing.

∽

The aroma of freshly brewed coffee pulled Logan out of his nightmare. It was the same one he'd been having for months. As usual, he woke up in a cold sweat. It took a minute for him to shake it off and remember he was home with the girls, all the girls, and everything was fine. Thankfully it wasn't like the last time when he'd yelled, and Alex had come in and woken him. Determined not to let it put a damper on his happiness or his plans for a fantastic weekend with Chloe, he grabbed a quick shower and headed downstairs. Hearing the girls carrying on in the kitchen, he wondered what act of God it had taken to keep them from waking him up.

"Good morning. How are all my girlies today?"

"Daddy. Yay." Bella jumped out of her chair and ran at him, knocking him hard enough that he almost lost his balance. Good thing he'd seen her coming and braced himself. She couldn't weigh more than forty pounds, but she packed a wallop.

"Bella, you need to finish your breakfast. Daddy needs his coffee." Bella made a face at her sister. He couldn't see it, but he could guess what it probably looked like. Not that he blamed her, Lexie was in little mother mode again.

"Lex, what did I tell you about bossing your sister?"

"Sorry, Mom."

Chloe nodded and handed Logan a steaming cup of nirvana, known as coffee to the rest of the world. Inhaling the scent helped to shake off the remnants of the dream. "Thanks, Princess."

Chloe smiled and gave him a kiss and a wink. "Good morning. I bet you've missed this, huh?"

"Hell yeah. Y'all are much better looking than the guys." He waggled his eyebrows. It made them laugh but it was too true. In his own kitchen, coffee in hand, and surrounded by his girls was a much better view. Pulling out a chair, he sat at the table.

"Daddy, you said a bad word. You have to

put money in the jar."

Logan looked at Chloe as she struggled to contain her laughter. "Umm, you're right. I need to watch that, don't I?"

Bella nodded as she shoveled another spoonful of cereal into her mouth.

"What's for breakfast?"

"I wanted pancakes, but mommy made me have Cheerios," Bella answered, screwing her face into a frown. "And no sugar either."

"Mom's a meany, huh?"

"Yes, she is."

"Hey, don't you start too. If she has too much sugar in the morning, I end up getting a call from her teacher that she's disrupting the class."

"Is that true, Bella?"

"Maybe." Logan hid his smile behind his coffee cup. Before he could get up, Chloe refilled it, and that's when he realized she didn't have a mug in front of her. He was about to ask when Lexie interrupted his train of thought.

"Do you want some Cheerios, Daddy?

"No thank you, Honey. I'm good with the coffee. When do we have to leave for school?"

Chloe glanced at the clock on the stove. "In

about a half hour."

"Did you tell them yet?"

Chloe shook her head as his words evaporated into the air and the girls zeroed in on him like a bullseye. He mouthed the words 'sorry' and she shrugged.

"I figured we'd wait until after school but go ahead and tell them now. Or they won't leave you alone."

"Tell us what?" Lexie asked.

"You know our anniversary is coming up, right? Remember we talked about it on Facetime the other night?" He waited for their nods before continuing. "Well, I'm going to take Mommy away for the weekend to celebrate."

"But what about us? Don't we get to go?"

"Not this time, Lex. Sorry, Sweetie. But we're not leaving until tomorrow, so we'll have lots of fun tonight."

"That's not fair. You just got home and now you're leaving again. Who's going to watch us?"

"Aunt Lily," Chloe answered, and was rewarded with an eye roll from Lexie worthy of an Academy Award. That kid was something else.

"What if we don't want her to?"

"Don't start. You always have fun with her, and I'm sure this time will be the same. We'll be back by the time you get home from school on Tuesday."

Bella got up from the table and whispered into Logan's ear, and he smiled. "Yes, Bella, I will." Chloe gave him a questioning look, but he shook his head, he'd fill her in later.

"Where are you going?" Lexie asked as she put her cereal bowl in the sink.

"To Sanibel Island, it's on the west coast on the Gulf of Mexico."

"Why do you have to go so far? We have the beach here."

"That's true. But the reason I'm home is that I have to talk to a bunch of other soldiers about what I do in Afghanistan. The meeting is near there."

"Oh. I guess that's okay then." He laughed. His daughters were definitely chips off the old block, and smarter than he expected for their age. But then what did he know, he hardly spent any time with them. A pang of regret tweaked his heart, but like so many other things, he buried it in the back of his mind. Now wasn't the time to dwell on anything but being with his family.

CHAPTER 5

As soon as Logan left with the girls, Chloe called Lily.

"Hey, girl. We surprised you, huh?"

"No shit. I don't know how you kept it quiet."

"It wasn't easy. Luckily, I had a lot of work to get done so it kept me busy."

"Speaking of that, are you going to be okay having the girls for four days? You've never watched them for that long."

"Eh, we'll be okay. Worst case, we'll go to the mall and I'll stuff them full of ice cream."

"Ugh, if you give Bella all that sugar, you'll be sorry. She'll never go to bed."

"That's okay, I've been stocking up on

Disney movies, we can have a marathon. Don't worry. It's not like I don't know them. I practically live at your house."

"True, but…"

"No buts. Just go and get laid, will you?"

"Bitch! And you're both crazy. What were you and Alex thinking? You spent way too much money."

"Nah. We wanted to do something special for you. It's your tenth anniversary—a big one. I've been dying to go there. Now you can tell me all about it when you get back. I'll drink wine and you can have water."

"You're really pushing it. But seriously, if you knew about this place, why haven't you and Alex gone yet?"

"We will one of these days. Maybe when he's home on leave next time. We'll see. It's not like we have to make arrangements for kids. We can just pick up and go." Chloe heard the hint of regret in her friend's voice. She almost wished it was Lily who'd gotten pregnant. They wanted a baby so badly. "Did you tell Logan about the baby?"

"No, not yet. I'm still deciding when to do it. I almost told him last night but then he hit me with the trip. Now I'm thinking about waiting until we get back."

"Why? Do you really think he'll be upset?"

"Honestly? I don't know. He seems overwhelmed by the girls. I know he's not used to them and they're not used to him either. Every time he comes home it's like a free for all because it's special. But what if he isn't happy? There will be more expenses, more responsibility, even if it's going to be on me."

"Yeah well about that, maybe you should ask him to reconsider re-upping for another deployment. I've been trying to convince Alex he should ask to be stationed stateside. They've put in their time. You know?"

"Yup, I do. But Logan always said that being deployed is the fastest way to move up through the ranks. So, what can I do? I feel like pushing him to stay here is sort of breaking our agreement. We knew what we were getting into, at least mostly. I didn't think he'd be gone so much."

"It's rough, more for you than me. It's lonely, like long distance dating. Neither one of them have been home long enough to know what day to day life is really like. But you have to know what I mean, right?"

"Yeah, I do."

"And what about the toll it's taking? They're living in constant danger, and when they finally get leave they're hardly here long enough to get all the sand off before they have to go back."

Lily was right, she'd get no argument from Chloe. She loved Logan and supported the choices he'd made over the years, but it didn't mean it wasn't hard on all of them. How many times had she reached for him in the middle of the night only to find cold sheets? And how much of the girls' lives had he missed? Sharing pictures afterward wasn't the same. Yeah, it was hard. But how could she ask him to choose his family over his career?

"What time are you dropping off the girls?"

"Logan said early. Probably around eight. Is that okay? It's going to take us close to four hours to get to Sanibel Island."

"Yeah, I'll probably still be in my jammies."

"Um, girlfriend, when aren't you in your PJs?"

"I wasn't when I picked up Logan yesterday. So there."

"Oh yeah, that's right. Shocking."

"It was a good thing too since we ran into

the colonel. I think Logan was worried I'd say something inappropriate."

"You? Nah, you'd never do that." Chloe laughed, she knew exactly what Lily meant and she could picture the look on his face. Lily was the queen of blurting out the wrong thing at the wrong time. It had made things interesting over the years.

"I'm trying to watch my mouth. But the look on your husband's face was hysterical. Oh yeah. That reminds me, make sure the girls leave that damn curse jar home. Last time Lexie brought it they bugged me the entire time. I told them it's okay to curse at my house."

"I heard all about it. Bella wanted to know why it was okay there but not here. I told them it was because you're an old lady who lives alone. But I'll make sure it stays here this time."

"Gee, thanks. Way to teach them to respect their elders."

"Sorry, but you cause enough damage hanging out in your pajamas all the time. Anyway, I'm gonna go. I need to pack, or at least try to figure out what to bring. Thank you again for everything and Alex too. I love you, girl."

"Love you, too. Just try to relax and have a

good time. Enjoy that sexy man while he's within reach."

"You know it."

When Logan returned from dropping the girls at school, she was upstairs with almost everything she owned strewn across the bed. All the 'mom' clothes were pushed out of the way since it was a grown-up trip. Her wardrobe wasn't equipped for adult activities. Not knowing what they were doing made it even harder. Would she need a dressy outfit? Then there was the shoe issue. She had sneakers and flip-flops. The only pair of heels she had were fifteen years old. Maybe she'd have time to run to the mall to pick up a few things before the girls got home.

"Are you bringing all of that? I was hoping you'd pack light, like only a bathing suit," he said and waggled his eyebrows.

"You're kidding right?"

"Not exactly. Swimming and sex sounds like the perfect weekend to me," he said as he pulled her into his arms. "Thank you for doing such a great job with our daughters. They're super kids."

Chloe smiled and wrapped her arms around his neck and slid her fingers through his close-cropped military haircut. She loved the bristly feel against her fingers. "Yes, they are, most of the time. Enough to keep me from killing them."

"Good thing, I wouldn't want to have to bail you out."

"Funny man. Seriously, though, you really don't expect me to just pack a bathing suit, do you? I was thinking of running to the mall. I don't have anything nice."

"I can dream, can't I?" He tilted her head up and stared into her eyes. Looking up at him, she got lost in his blue-purple eyes. She'd never seen anything like it before she'd met him. And then there were his long dark eyelashes. What she wouldn't have given for those? Her gaze widened and the fine lines at the corners of his eyes made her sad. They hadn't been there at Christmas. Too much sun or stress. Either way, he looked exhausted. Maybe they should take a nap while the girls were in school.

Before she had a chance to reply, he rubbed his lips against hers. The kiss gentle, almost reverent. Then drawing back, he smiled and pulled out the clip holding her hair up and watched as it fell down around her shoulders. The second kiss wasn't gentle at all. His body shook as his tongue swept the inside of her mouth and he groaned against her lips.

Walking her backward until her legs hit the edge of the bed, he shoved the piles of clothing onto the floor then lowered her onto the mattress. Settling next to her, he lifted her t-shirt and his fingertips traced patterns on her stomach. Then he pulled her into his arms for an even more passionate kiss. Needing to feel his skin against her, craving the contact she'd missed for months, she pulled on his t-shirt until he pulled it over his head with one hand giving her what she wanted. Her hands skimmed over him, relearning every curve and dip of his muscled chest.

With another groan, he released her lips. Filled with passion, his eyes darkened to violet. She knew that look. Her body recognized it too. Her panties were soaked, and the corners of his lips curled in a sexy smile that said he knew it.

Without saying a word, they undressed, tossing their clothes, desperate with need. His passion ignited and fanned the flames of her arousal. Each touch pushed her closer to release as his fingers painted a trail of fire down her body. Moaning, she arched up against him to get closer, needing more of him. But he wasn't letting her have any control, and he didn't stop until she screamed his name.

∽

Chloe was going to be the death of him. From the first time they were together it was like they were two halves of one whole, and her response to his touch never failed to amaze him. If anyone had told him twelve years ago that he'd still be head over heels for the same woman he'd have laughed in their face. Yet, there he was, still burning with an all-consuming need to possess every inch of her. As if she could read her mind, she wrapped her legs around him and squeezed, and all thought fled as his orgasm rocked him to his core.

Her soft breaths should have lulled him to sleep, but his mind wouldn't shut down. Instead it ran through scenarios and discarded them as quickly as they became thoughts. He was so close to advancement which meant more pay. More money would make life easier for them, but was it worth it? He wasn't there to see his daughters grow up, and the woman he loved more than life itself was spending most of their marriage alone.

A muffled buzz caught his attention. Once he realized it was his phone, he had to find the damn thing. It had been in the pocket of his jeans when he'd tossed them somewhere in the pile of clothing. Gently sliding out from under Chloe, he tried not to wake her. Then he searched the pile of his, hers, and what she'd been going through to pack. It was crazy, but it made him laugh. The jeans were at the bottom of the pile, but he finally located them from the beeping. Grabbing it and his pants, he quietly left the bedroom.

In the hallway, he unlocked the screen to check the missed calls. Hoping it wasn't the captain or the colonel, he was happy to see it was the hotel. Figuring they were confirming his reservation, he didn't bother to listen to the voicemail and instead hit redial.

"White Sands Resort & Spa, Katie speaking."

"Hi, this is Logan Mitchell. Someone there just called me?"

"Ah yes, Lt. Mitchell. I was calling to confirm your reservation for tomorrow and your wife's spa appointment for Monday."

"Great. We should be arriving sometime in the early afternoon."

"No problem, sir. If your suite isn't ready we will check your baggage and you can enjoy a meal or explore the island."

"Excellent. Do you have the order for the flowers and champagne?"

"Yes, sir. They'll be waiting in your suite."

"Thank you. This is going to be a wonderful anniversary celebration."

"Yes, Sir. See you tomorrow."

No sooner had he hung up when the bedroom door opened, and a tousle-haired Chloe peeked out. "What's going on?" she asked as she yawned.

"I'm sorry, I tried not to wake you. It was the resort confirming our reservations for tomorrow."

"You shouldn't have let me sleep. I have so much to do, like getting us packed before the kids come home and running to the mall to pick up a few things. I was thinking that if we spend the entire evening with them, it'll ease the sting when we leave them at Lily's tomorrow."

"For them or you?"

"I'll miss them, but not as much as I'm going to love a weekend alone with my sex-god hunky husband."

"Sex-god huh? Princess, you have no idea."

"No? You been reading how-to books in the desert?"

"Ha. Like I need the help."

"I should have kept my mouth shut. Your head is big enough already."

Lifting her into his arms he kissed her hard. He'd hoped to take her breath away and let her get to her to do list, instead he had to have her again. After he teased her to release twice more he thrust into her fast and hard until he thought his heart would explode with the force of his orgasm.

"Sexy enough for you, Princess?"

"Uh huh, where did that come from?"

"I have to make up for lost time."

"I'll say. I'm not sure I'll be able to walk after this weekend."

"Good." His shit-eating grin earned him a smack across his chest. "Don't worry about packing for me, I'll throw my trunks and some shorts in my bag. Just take care of you."

"No dress slacks?"

"I'll throw in a pair of those and a nice shirt. Okay?"

"If we're not going anywhere nice, then don't."

Logan smiled, she was trying hard to figure

out what he had planned, but he knew all her tricks and was determined to keep them a secret. "It never hurts to be prepared."

"You're not going to tell me anything are you?"

"Nope. You should know better after all of these years."

"It never hurts to try. Thank you, Love, for all of this. And thank you for earlier," she said with a wink as color suffused her cheeks and her eyes twinkled with mischief. He loved her playful side, and he hoped to see a lot more of it over the next few days.

A smile and two strides later he pulled her into his arms again for a toe-curling kiss. As usual, he couldn't keep his hands off her, but for some reason it was more of a need than ever before. Maybe it was her extra glow, or maybe it was all the stress catching up to him.

"By the way, what did Bella whisper earlier," Chloe asked after she caught her breath.

Logan laughed. His daughter was a piece of work. "She asked me to bring home a little sister, so she could boss her around like Lexie does to her."

"She didn't."

"Hell yeah, she did. She's a trip."

"More like a little mini-you." Chloe had a strange look on her face, but it was only there for a second or two before she started weeding through the clothing strewn all over their bedroom.

CHAPTER 6

After dropping their two sleepy daughters at Lily's they hopped onto I-95 north to begin their escape. Four hours later they exited I-75 south. There was only a three-mile drive over the causeway to Sanibel Island and then a short drive to the resort. Chloe had slept most of the drive and was surprised when Logan didn't call her on it. It was unusual for her to sleep in the car, but they hadn't been on a road trip in a while so maybe he didn't remember.

Deciding if and when to tell him about the baby was still weighing heavy on her so much that she'd been dreaming about it. She couldn't even say why she was hesitating. Of course, he'd be happy. He loved the girls. There was no reason in the world he wouldn't be as thrilled as she was to have another one. But what if he wasn't happy? It was freaking her out that she had doubts at all. She should have just blurted it out when he'd told her about Bella's whispered request, but something stopped her. She needed to pull up her big girl panties and just tell him. It was stupid. Logan had always been her Prince Charming and never let her down, so there was no reason to think he would be anything other than ecstatic. So how come her stomach knotted up whenever she thought about telling him?

"It's breathtaking isn't it?" Chloe said as she gazed through the car window at the turquoise blue water. It looked fake it was so blue, but she was used to the green-blue of the Atlantic Ocean.

"Yes, it is. Are you feeling okay? I should have let you get more sleep last night." Logan glanced at her before returning his focus to the road. Oops. He did realize something was off. Still, she wasn't going to blurt it out in the car. There had to be a better time. Then she saw the sign for White Sands Resort & Spa. "Woo hoo. Look. We're almost there."

"Thank God. I can't wait to stretch my legs.

I should have stopped at a rest area, but you were sleeping so peacefully I didn't want to wake you."

"You should have stopped anyway, Honey."

"I will in about ten minutes," he said and chuckled. God, how she loved him. He was the other half of her heart. She doubted he realized how hard it was to watch him leave each time. Taking her heart and leaving her with a hollow emptiness that lingered until he returned. The emptiness was always there, but she'd never noticed it as sharply as when she had looked up to see him standing in the kitchen doorway.

The resort grounds distracted her from her thoughts. Still in the same state but it was like they'd gone through a wormhole and ended up in paradise. There were flowers and flowering plants everywhere. Pink and white oleanders and hibiscus in bright red and pink were just the beginning. "It's gorgeous, Logan. I can't believe we're staying here."

"It really is. I guess we're going to owe Alex and Lily big time."

"No kidding. But it will be so worth it."

"After seeing the look on your face, I'd gladly give Alex anything," Logan said and smiled after he pulled up to the valet stand in front of the hotel.

They'd stayed in nice hotels but nothing like this. It was like being one of the rich and famous as the valet came around and opened her door. As she stood up and stepped away from the car every muscle in her body thanked her. Looking around, trying to take everything in, she almost laughed. They were away, together, alone in paradise. If she'd smiled any wider her face would probably crack.

The valet took their car keys and grabbed their luggage from the trunk and put in on a cart. "We'll take care of this for you. When your room is ready we'll deliver it."

Chloe elbowed Logan, and when he looked at her, she pointed to her purse. He reached into his pocket and pulled out his wallet.

"Thank you, the name's Mitchell," Logan replied, and handed the valet a five dollar bill. She hoped it was enough, it was like they were hicks with no idea how to play in this world. The lobby was beautiful, more plants, flowers and several sitting areas. As they made their way to check-in, it was every bit as beautiful as the pictures on their website. A pretty strawberry-blonde woman greeted them when they stopped at the reservation desk.

"Hello and welcome to the White Sands Resort & Spa. My name is Katie and I'll be happy to help with anything you need."

"Hi, Katie. We're the Mitchells, Logan and Chloe."

She smiled as she pulled up their information on the computer. "We're glad to have you with us. Oh, I see it's your tenth anniversary. Congratulations."

"But how did…" Chloe started to ask then realized it had to be Lily's plotting again or maybe Logan's. Nah. He wasn't that romantic, was he? "Yes, it is. Thank you."

Katie placed a map of the property on the counter and gave them a quick explanation of the grounds, the restaurants, and where their suite was located. The resort was huge, over twenty-three acres and so much to do they could have stayed a couple of weeks and not been able to do and see everything. They'd have to find some way to thank Lily and Alex for this because it was amazeballs.

"If you need anything just call the front desk. I hope you enjoy your stay."

"Thank you, I'm sure we will."

Logan took her hand and led the way to their building. He was just as handsome as he'd been on their wedding day, older, a few grays, but her heart still jumped for joy every time he was near. And now she had him to herself for a whole weekend. Everything would work out as long as they had each other.

∼

The resort was everything Logan had hoped for and more. Seeing Chloe's face glowing with excitement warmed his heart. As they walked to the suite she chattered on just like Lexie. Since he'd been home she'd been constantly exhausted, and it worried him. Usually, she was a ball of energy. Instead of registering super-sonic on the excitement gauge for like this trip, she'd fallen asleep almost as soon as they'd hit the highway. It was very unlike her and after they got back home he was going to try to get her to see the doctor. But for now, it was going to be seventy-two hours of fun in the sun.

Unlocking the door to their suite, he scooped her into his arms and carried her across the threshold, just as he had ten years earlier when they had gotten married. He was proud of himself for thinking to do it but being around Chloe brought out his romantic side. Kicking the door closed behind them, he kissed her before setting her on her feet. The suite was larger than their first apartment and decorated a hell of a lot nicer. It had everything they could possibly need, even a gas grill on the patio. With a little imagination, it would be easy to believe they'd left the country and traveled to a far-off exotic land.

"Wow. I didn't see that coming."

"I still have a few surprises up my sleeve."

"Logan?"

"Hmm?"

"You're not wearing sleeves, not long ones, so it would be kinda hard to hide something up there." She giggled and looked just like she did when he met her in college.

"You're a funny woman. But you'll see."

"I guess we will. This is gorgeous. I can't believe we're actually here. Oh my God. Best anniversary ever."

"And we're just getting started."

A knock on the door stopped him from undressing her right there. The bellman carried their suitcases into the bedroom, while he and Chloe explored the rest of the suite. This time he remembered on his own to tip him. He'd just closed the door when he heard her screech. His 'instant on' took over, and he followed the sound of her voice expecting to see a snake or some kind of animal threatening to harm his wife.

"What the hell, Chloe, you scared the shit out of me."

"Sorry. But look?" She was holding a huge basket filled with fruit, cheese, crackers, and chocolate. "The card says, 'Happy Anniversary, compliments of the staff at White Sands Resort & Spa.' How awesome is that?"

Grinning, he took the basket and placed it on the table and pulled her into his arms. If she was excited now wait until she saw the champagne and flowers waiting for her in the bedroom.

"I love you, Mrs. Mitchell. You're the reason I wake up every day. I hope you know that no matter how far away I am when I open my eyes in the morning you're the first person I think of and always will be." He hadn't intended to make her cry, but her eyes welled up with tears. Holding her face in his hands, he wiped them away with his thumb and touched his lips to hers.

A gentle kiss was all he intended but once again their passion flared and as soon as they touched the fire ignited and raced down his spine. With a groan, he carried her into the bedroom. Pulling back the covers, he deposited her on the bed with a bounce and a smile.

Chloe's surprise quickly turned to desire. Her cheeks flushed a lovely shade of rose and her expression mesmerized him. As she sat up and began to unbutton her blouse, he stopped her and grabbed a rose out of the vase by the side of the bed and handed it to her.

"I love you, Princess. I hope this makes up for missing so many things."

A huge smile spread across her face. "I love you, Babe. And yes, this is all amazing."

"Good. Now hands off. Undressing you is my job."

"You waited too long," she said and tossed her shirt at him.

"Game on." Pulling his polo shirt over his head, he kicked off his sneakers and dropped his shorts. He was rewarded with her indrawn breath when she realized he'd gone commando.

"Do you do that often?" She asked as she licked her lips.

"Nope, only for you, Princess." It was his

turn to groan as she wrapped her soft hands around him and caressed his throbbing cock.

"I meant not wear your boxers, silly. It better only happen for me." He laughed but the time for conversation was over, and soon they were lost in each other.

○○○

After unpacking, they changed into their bathing suits and went out to the pool. The late afternoon sun reflected on the pool surface like a thousand tiny diamonds and took Chloe's breath away. It was probably hormones, but everything about this place filled her with happiness, or maybe it was having Logan all to herself. It was the best present of all. She'd been completely serious when she'd said an overnight stay in the Holiday Inn outside of town would have been fantastic. She loved her children more than anything. But being alone with the man who owned her heart? There just wasn't anything better.

"What are you thinking about, Princess?"

"You, the girls, how beautiful it is here. And you some more." He grinned, and she loved how his eyes crinkled at the corners. They were getting older, but definitely better, as the last couple of hours proved.

"Do you want to do anything this afternoon, or just relax?"

"I think relaxing by the pool with that basket of snacks sounds like an excellent idea."

"I can take the hint, be right back." She watched as he walked back to their building and up the stairs to their suite. His body had changed from their college days; it was more solid—muscular—but life had taken its toll on him too. The six-inch scar on his right shoulder reminded her of the danger he lived with every day. She tried not to dwell on what his life was like when he was away from then. It was the life of a military spouse and if she worried all the time she'd end up in a padded room.

The pool called to her. It had been forever since she'd been in one, most of her water time was a shower these days or the ocean with the girls when they had time. The water was warm as a bath, she'd forgotten how much pools heated in the summer. That was Florida life, even the 'cold' water from the faucet was warm in the summer months. The Gulf would be warm too, though not quite as warm as the pool.

"How is it?" Logan asked as he returned with his arms full of snacks and a couple of water bottles. She was glad he hadn't grabbed the bottle of wine. He knew she loved it and turning it down would definitely have triggered questions.

"Perfect. How about snacks in the pool instead of beside it?"

"Works for me."

When she'd put on her suit, she was surprised to see how much of a baby bump was showing. She probably shouldn't have been since it was her third pregnancy and she was over four months along. Still, she'd hoped the fabric would have hidden more. The transition to maternity clothes was not high on her happy list and she hoped to put it off for as long as possible. It also reinforced the need to tell Logan before he went back to Afghanistan.

He handed her a bottle of water. As his fingers brushed against her hand a tingle of need raced along her nerve endings setting off little shocks of desire. From the look on his face, he must have felt it too. It was like being in college again, when they couldn't keep their hands off each other.

As the afternoon passed they basked in the

sunshine, laughing, sharing cheese and crackers, and pieces of fruit. Stealing kisses in between laughing about her stories of the girl's antics over the last few months. Happiness filled her soul, and she made the decision she'd tell him about the baby tomorrow. Today would just be about relaxing and just enjoying each other.

CHAPTER 7

Logan stepped off the edge and into the pool, diving into the warm water to touch the bottom. Coming up for air next to Chloe, he shook the water off his face. For a moment he thought she was asleep. Eyes closed, arms resting on the pool edge, just floating like some kind of siren. The sun caught the red highlights in her hair and kissed her skin with a golden glow. In her turquoise swimsuit and mostly submerged in the water, she could have passed for a mermaid. She'd certainly captivated him.

"Hey, Princess."

"Mmm. Hi, lover boy. It's so peaceful here. Like we have our own private pool."

"I know. It's amazing. I bet most people are

at the beach. The island is known for being one of the best spots for shell collecting. But I'm not complaining, with no machine gun fire, and no kids to interrupt us…hell it doesn't get much better."

Her eyes popped open, and she gave him an odd look, almost like worry. What had he said? Was it the machine gun reference? Maybe she was thinking about when he would head back.

"I wonder what the girls are doing right now."

"Probably terrorizing Lily."

"Maybe. Or she might be terrorizing them." Thinking about Lily running around chasing after the girls in her fuzzy bunny slippers made them laugh, and he was happy to see her frown disappear.

"I hope she gets pregnant the next time Alex comes home. She wants a baby so much."

"Maybe we can give them one of ours. It would make life easier if you only had one wouldn't it?" A shadow slid across her face and she looked sad. Somehow, he'd upset her. How he'd done it, he didn't have a clue. But it was time to step away before he really stuck his foot in his mouth. "I'm going to do a couple of laps. I don't want to lose this trim physique." Giving her a quick kiss, he turned and slid through the water.

The steady strokes helped him think. Water always had. He wasn't sure why or when he realized it, but it worked. Even showers helped when he had to reason out a problem. But this time even after six laps, he still couldn't figure out what he'd said to upset Chloe. She was usually so easy going. Something had to be bothering her, she should be relaxed just being in the peace and quiet. At home he could understand, the girls probably got to her after a while, but here, she should be relaxed and happy. Was he being a typical male and missing all the clues?

Not finding any answers, he came up for air and decided the easiest solution was the most direct. He'd just ask if he'd upset her and what he could do to fix it. The last thing he wanted was to ruin their time together. But she wasn't there. Not in the pool or on the patio. Warning bells rang in his head. Too bad he didn't know what the hell he'd done, but there was no doubt in his mind he'd done something. Grabbing one of the towels, he hurried up to their suite. Might as well tackle it head on and get it settled. He'd grovel at her feet if that's what it took to put the smile back on her face.

~

Watching Logan's arms slice through the water was like watching poetry in motion. There wasn't anything he didn't excel at, from sports to Trivial Pursuit, to making love. But after his remark about giving one of their daughters to Lily, even if it was supposed to be a joke, she couldn't shake off the dread that he was going to be unhappy when he found out about the baby. Waiting until after they got back home sounded like a better idea as each minute passed. She was such a chicken shit. But they needed this weekend together, it happened so rarely. For all she knew it might be another ten years before they'd go away alone again. What harm could there be in waiting a few more days? Decision made she felt a little better. Kind of. Sort of.

She was never good at putting things out of her mind. Instead she dwelled on stuff, worried it to death until she came up with a solution. It was one of the few things they repeatedly fought over during their marriage. Stress was her middle name while he was calm and level-headed. It was a good balance, except at times like this.

Not sure how long he'd be swimming, she got out of the pool, grabbed some crackers, and went inside to take a shower. With the girls still in school, they hadn't spent a lot of time in the sun yet and her skin was turning a light shade of pink. The last thing she needed was sunburn, but the bit of color made her look less tired.

As the water rained over her body, she thought about how she'd tell Logan about the baby. It could go a few ways. The outcome she wanted was for him to be thrilled and decide that he didn't need to do another deployment. If he'd ask for a permanent assignment at Fitzsimmons, her life would be perfect. But she couldn't ask him to give up career advancement for them. He'd worked hard and made many sacrifices to get where he wanted in his career. They had too. The girls had to live with an absentee father and she with an absentee husband. Being a single parent sucked wind, but at least he came home. She had too many friends whose husbands would never return. Just thinking about that scared the shit out of her.

"Who are you talking to?"

"What?" Startled by Logan's voice in the bathroom, she almost slipped. Was she talking out loud? Crap. What had she said?

"You were talking. I thought you were on the phone until I heard the shower. As far as I can tell you're alone in there. I'd be happy to remedy that situation if you'd like?"

"C'mon in. I was singing. I thought I was doing it under my breath, but I guess I got carried away."

"Okay," he said as he chuckled. "When you weren't still in the pool, I was worried I'd pissed you off or that you were sick."

"Nah. Everything is fine. My shoulders started to feel hot and I figured it was time to go inside or have the chef think one of his lobsters had escaped."

"Good. I prefer my wife in non-lobster form."

"That's what I thought too." Giggling, she playfully punched him in the stomach, and he pretended to be mortally wounded. Then he scooped her into his arms and held her under the shower head.

"Put me down, brute."

"No way. You're my prisoner now. What

should I do with you, hmmm?" Turning them around so the water ran over his back and not over her head, he grinned. It didn't take long to change from playful to seductive as he took possession of her mouth. His tongue swept inside, and their tongues dueled in a dance they'd practiced for years.

His hands traveled her body, she thanked God he was holding her since her knees gave out. He knew all the spots that drove her wild. Without breaking the kiss, he settled her onto his cock and coaxed her legs around his hips. She slid her hands over his shoulders but stopped at the roughened skin of his scar.

As if he knew what she was thinking, he spoke against her lips, "Stop, don't think about it. I'm here now." He was right, live in the moment. Lily told her that time and again, but it wasn't an easy thing for her to do. But Logan knew her too well. Sliding one of his rough fingertips over her clit cleared her mind of anything but him, and when he bit her lip all coherent thought dissipated like smoke in the wind.

~

"Why don't we have dinner in the suite tonight. It's been a long day. You must be tired. I know I'm exhausted. This way you don't have to get dressed up. Unless you want to?"

"It's a perfect idea. I bet there's enough stuff in the basket to feed us without ordering anything."

"Maybe for you but I'm a growing man."

Laughing, Chloe threw a pillow at him. "Seriously? What's growing on you except your beer belly."

"Hey, I don't have a beer belly." To prove it, he ripped off the towel that was tucked around his waist. Catching his reflection in the mirror, he turned sideways to check. "Besides," he said as he waggled his eyebrows. "I think you just experienced what grows." He loved that she still blushed, and as the color raced up her chest to her cheeks it was like seeing the sun set over the ocean, the slow crawl of color until the entire sky was painted pink.

"Whatever."

"Thems fighting words. You don't want to go back into the shower, do you?"

"Don't you dare. I'm already waterlogged and wrinkly." Raising his eyebrows, he winked at her. She knew that look and she made a run for it. He chased her and pushed her down on the bed and tickled her until she collapsed in a fit of giggles. This was the Chloe he'd fallen in love with, snarky, shy, and incredibly passionate. He couldn't have asked for a more perfect partner.

Pulling on a t-shirt and a pair of shorts, he followed her into the main room of the suite. She'd already set out the rest of the food from the gift basket.

"You found us a feast."

"Yeah, this place is beyond impressive. The bath products. Oh my God. They sell them at the spa. I might have to get some to bring home."

"Sure. You can pick some up when you're having your spa day on Monday. Surprise. I arranged for a full day of Chloe pampering while I'm at MacDill."

"Seriously? You did not." She hugged him so hard it took his breath away.

"I see where the girls get it from now."

"Huh? Oh, sorry."

"Don't you dare. I love that I've made you so happy. It was the plan. Lily and Alex might have started it, but I wanted to make sure you really enjoyed this weekend. I don't pamper you nearly enough."

"I am, Baby. You have no idea."

"I think I might have a little idea."

"No, you don't."

"Are we going to start this again?"

"Only if you can catch me."

"Damn, I should have brought one of the kid's super soakers. You'd be sorry then."

"Neener, neener. Too bad you didn't think of it before. Now you're out of luck."

"Don't underestimate me, I'm a well-trained soldier of the United States of America. We are always prepared."

"Well, soldier. Why don't you sit your butt down and eat and then we can walk on the beach and watch the sunset."

"Yes, ma'am."

Soft music played as they enjoyed their dinner. Once again feeding each other, and this time it was Logan's turn to tell Chloe what he could of his life in Afghanistan. After he shared his stories of sand storms and some of the people he'd met, she told him about the leak. He couldn't stop laughing when she told him about the look on Lexie's face as the water shot up like a fountain.

"I'm glad you think it's funny, you didn't have to clean it up. And the plumber guy that Lily recommended? Holy crap. What a freakin' character. But at least he was cheap."

"That's good. Remind me to take a look at it when we get home."

When then were full they cleared up what was left and headed out to the beach. All of the suites were just a short walk to the water, and soon they were digging their toes in the sand.

Chloe had left her hair down, and the wind was blowing it around her face. He loved it this way, but when she was in mommy-mode she kept it in a ponytail or clipped with one of those alligator clips. As they walked the beach, holding hands, they passed several other couples and even families collecting seashells and waiting for the sunset. Shades of golds, pinks, and purples painted the sky as the sun slid into the Gulf leaving behind lavender and violets as the evening sky took over.

In the fading light, as she stood at the water's edge, he was taken aback by her beauty. She practically glowed. When she caught him staring, she kicked sand in his direction. "C'mon help me find some more shells, they're the cheapest souvenirs we're going to get."

"This is the seashell capital of Florida. I'm sure if we come out in the morning there will be plenty to find. It's amazing what you can see when the sun is out," he said with a smirk. Lucky for him that she'd been concentrating on her shell search or he'd have ended up in the water.

"The moon is almost full, there's plenty of light."

Another couple walked by and greeted them as they continued down the beach. The man was wearing a shirt from the Ding Darling Wildlife Refuge and it reminded him he'd meant to make reservations for tomorrow. He'd totally forgotten earlier. He wanted to rent a boat to take her to Ding Darling. When he'd looked through the information for Sanibel Island he'd read all about it and thought she'd love it. He needed to call the front desk and see if they could still make arrangements for tomorrow.

"Why don't we go back to the suite. I want to see if I can rent a boat tomorrow to take you to the wildlife refuge. It's supposed to be amazing."

"Really? I didn't know there was one around here."

"Yup. Are you up for it?"

"Sure, it sounds like fun. I can add it to my bucket list. Private romantic boat tour of a wildlife refuge. I wonder how private it'll be?"

"You wonder huh? Since when do you have a bucket list?"

"Duh, Logan, it's not like we haven't talked about it." They had? He didn't recall her ever saying anything about a bucket list. Was she sure it wasn't some other Logan?

By the time they got back to the suite it was dark. The lights had come on by the pool illuminating it with blues and greens. Once in the room he called the front desk and was thrilled to be able to reserve a boat for the morning. He booked it for ten figuring that gave them plenty of time to wake up and grab something to eat before driving over. It was a vacation after all.

"You up for some champagne, Princess?"

"Nah, I'm beat and if I have that now I'll be out cold in no time. Let's save it. Unless you want a glass?" She yawned as she answered. All the fresh sea air after the long drive was making them both tired. She probably was right about the champagne. Better to save it for their anniversary toast on Monday evening. He couldn't wait to spring that surprise on her.

CHAPTER 8

Startled awake from a deep sleep, Chloe squinted at the bedside clock. Three a.m.? What woke her?

"Incoming. Take cover. Dammit, Sherm, get the fuck out of there. Now."

Logan was thrashing in the bed. Not sure what to do, she tentatively touched the arm closest to her, ready to jump out of bed if he went on the attack. Lily had told her that once Alex had punched her when she'd woken him from a nightmare. He'd felt horrible and told her to just let him wake up on his own if it happened again. But they were in a hotel and she didn't know how soundproof it was. The last thing she needed was security at their door.

"Goddammit, incoming. Medic. We need a fucking medic."

Her light touch didn't have an effect. She tried again, shaking him this time. "Logan, wake up. You're having a dream. C'mon on, Baby. It's okay," she murmured using the same tone she did when the girls had nightmares. He stopped yelling but was still thrashing around.

He'd told her about Sherm. He'd been eighteen when he was killed in action last year, barely out of high school. His life was cut way too short and Chloe had grieved for him and his family. It had hit Logan hard, as had every loss, but she hadn't realized he'd been having nightmares about it.

"Logan?"

"I'm awake. What's wrong? Are you okay?"

"I'm fine. You were having a nightmare." All she got was a grunt. "Are you really awake."

"Yeah. Sorry, Princess. I get them on and off. I was hoping they'd go away now that I'm at home."

"Do you want to talk about it?"

"I've been trying to ignore them."

"That doesn't seem to be working too well."

"You don't need to hear all the gory details."

"Now I understand why you look so exhausted. When was the last time you slept through the night?" The mattress shifted as he turned to face her, but she couldn't see more than the outline of his body. She almost turned on the light. But imagining the tortured expression he'd be wearing was hard enough. Seeing it would break her heart.

"I didn't mean to wake you."

"Babe, it's fine. You didn't do it on purpose. But since I am awake, I'm going to get some water. Do you want anything?"

"I'll get up too. Let's go sit on the patio. I need to get outside." After a bathroom stop, she grabbed a couple of water bottles and stepped onto the patio. Logan was sitting on one of the chaise lounges with his head in his hands. Her first instinct was to rush over and hug him, but she knew better. He wouldn't want her pity, support yes, pity no, and he'd think that's what it was.

"Here you go." She handed him a bottle and sat down in the other chair. Except for the occasional frog, it was so quiet that she could hear the ocean lapping against the shoreline. The star-filled sky engulfed their little piece of paradise in a sparkling blanket. It would have been magical if not for the reason they were awake in the middle of the night. Waiting and hoping he'd open up to her was heartbreaking. He had to know she wouldn't judge him, that she was his safe haven. At least she hoped he did.

All the waiting while he was turning it over and over in his head was driving her mad. He needed to just spit it out and she was on the verge of trying to pry it out of him when he took a swig of water. Then turned to face her.

"Could you understand what I said?"

"I heard Sherm's name."

"Fuck." He sighed, rubbed his hands over his head and took another swig of water. Then his eyes met hers, and there was just enough moonlight to see his face, and it was devastating. The stark anguish brought tears to her eyes, but she fought to blink them back. The last thing he needed was her tears.

"It's okay, you know. In sickness and in health, until death do us part. Remember?"

"Yeah, but you don't need to hear my horror stories."

"I do. The last few times you've been home I've felt like there was a wall between us. You're distancing yourself from all of us. I thought it was because you've been away so much. But now I think it's this. You're holding all this shit in and cutting yourself off from me or maybe everyone. Have you at least talked to Alex?"

"He knows but we haven't talked about it."

"Why not? Don't you think he has them too? I know he does. I was kind of surprised I'd never heard you have one. But maybe you weren't sleeping deeply enough."

A sheepish look came over his face. He averted his eyes and gazed into the darkness. She had no idea what was going through his mind. But whatever it was made him shudder.

"You know, I kind of understand your reluctance to share your feelings, but you have to talk to someone. If you don't let it out, it's going to eat you alive. Actually, I think it already is."

Another sigh escaped as he met her eyes. The tortured expression was gone and was replaced with resolve. "You're right about all of it. I should be strong enough to handle it, but when I wasn't I couldn't admit it to anyone. Sherm's death hit me hard. There were others before and since, but he was different. Maybe because he was so young, fuck he didn't even shave yet. Being in that Godforsaken hellhole was the last place he should have been."

Chloe nodded but kept silent. She was afraid if she interrupted him he'd stop talking and he needed this, no matter how hard it might be for her to hear.

"Did you know his mother wrote to me afterward?" She shook her head; still not sure she should speak. "She did. Wanted to tell me how grateful she was for me being so great to her son. Apparently, he'd written and told her all about me like I was some kind of fucking hero. What kind of hero lets an eighteen-year-old get blown to bits? They couldn't even find all of him. I'll never forget the look on his face as he turned to me as the bomb exploded."

She couldn't let him keep blaming himself. It was war, he didn't start it and he sure as hell wasn't going to be the one to end it. Too many people died, and they were all too young. But it sure as shit wasn't his fault. She moved over to his chaise and wrapped her arms around his waist as she leaned against his back.

"I know you did all you could to save him—to save them all. It's how you're made. It's what makes you so good at your job."

"I should have been able to save him."

"Babe, you can't save everyone. I can't believe you've been carrying this around with you for over a year and blaming yourself. Logan, look at me. It's not your fault about Sherm, Mac, Tag, or any of the guys. It just is. You have to let it go." At first, she wasn't sure he'd heard her. But then he pulled her onto his lap.

"I know. It makes sense in my brain, but in my heart? That's another story."

"You're looking at it wrong."

"How am I doing that? A kid is dead. Shit, hundreds maybe thousands of kids are dead. And yeah, he might have been over eighteen, but he was still a kid. I don't think he'd even been with a woman yet."

"Trust me, you are. His mother wrote to you because you helped her son when she couldn't, you mentored him, gave him the strength to deal with what he had to. By doing that you gave her the strength to deal with his loss. She knew he didn't die alone, and he was cared for. You have no idea how important that is to a mother. Don't you see that?"

"I never looked at it that way."

Chloe's lips curved into a gentle smile, one she'd often used with the girls. Being a mother had taught her a lot of people skills, and she was grateful she could use them to help Logan.

One of his large callused hands slid under her hair and along her neck, he tilted her head back and lowered his lips for a kiss. She tasted his regret but also relief. It convinced her more than ever that it was time for him to come home permanently.

"Babe, I know that this is the life you've chosen, but it might be time to reconsider everything. For a change..."

"What? Quit?"

"No, not quit. Just not go on any more deployments. You've done more than your share."

"Chloe." He sounded exasperated. Not exactly the reaction she'd hoped for, but what she should have expected. "We talked about this. You know it's the best opportunity for advancement. I want to provide a good life for you and the girls."

"I understand that I really do. But what about the toll it's taking on you? On all of us? Don't you think they'd rather have you home? Do you really believe any of us care whether you're a lieutenant, captain, or a colonel?"

"I care."

"I know you do," she said with a sigh. She was fighting a losing battle. "I don't want to argue over this, I don't. I just hate seeing how this is eating you alive. I love you, Logan. You're the man of my dreams, and I don't want to lose you. Will you at least think about it? Please?"

"You're not going to lose me."

"You don't know that for sure. Every time you leave, it could be for the last time. Look at what we're talking about. It could just as easily have been you instead of Sherm. Or what about Mac and Tag, and the Humvee. How many close calls have you had over the years? Don't even try to tell me you haven't. I've seen enough wives get notified, every time one of those damn military cars pulls up in front of someone's house it tears us all up."

"But you've known this was my life—our life—from the beginning."

"Yes. That's true. I did. But I didn't realize it would mean I'd have to raise the girls on my own. If I didn't have Lily I don't know how I would have handled it." Storm clouds gathered in his eyes and she knew she'd gone too far. But like a runaway train, she couldn't stop. Obviously, he wasn't the only one with bottled-up issues.

"I knew it would be a mistake to talk to you

about this. That you'd make it into something it's not. I feel horrible, yes. But you're right, I need to let it go, and you're overreacting. Seriously, Chloe. I'm fine, I'll be fine. We'll be fine. You'll see."

Before she could stop herself, the words popped out and lay between them like an elephant in the room. "I'm pregnant." Shit, not exactly her finest moment. And definitely not how she planned on breaking the news. As she waited and watched for a sign, her stomach was tied up in knots. But there was no reaction, nothing to show he was happy or upset about the news. Maybe he hadn't heard her. It was stupid, they loved each other, growing their family was a wonderful blessing. He had to think that, didn't he?

Finally, after what felt like an hour but was closer to a minute, he swallowed, and looked like he was searching for words. Seeing that he didn't seem happy with the news was her fear coming to life before her eyes. Pulling out of his embrace she got to her feet. The last thing she wanted was to be in his arms if he was going to say something to piss her off. She needed breathing room.

CHAPTER 9

"You're pregnant?"
"Yes. I found out three days ago. I'm about four months along. Apparently, you gave me an extra Christmas present when you were home." She'd moved to the edge of the balcony and faced him with her arms wrapped around her waist like she was protecting the baby. Her body language screamed for him to take her into his arms. To tell her everything would be alright. But he couldn't, he physically could not move, like he'd been cemented to the chair. Holy fuck. Another baby. He was going to be a dad again. A myriad of emotions raced through his mind. They were going to have another baby. He was happy, damn happy. So

why was she staring at him like she expected him to lose it?

"This is great news. A baby. It also explains a lot. You've been sleeping so much I was worried you were sick. Especially when you fell asleep in the car."

"I wondered if you'd noticed, and nope, I'm definitely not sick. But I am about to get really huge again."

"I love it when you're pregnant. You're adorable."

"You're not upset?"

"Upset? Why...oh Princess, did you really think I'd be upset? You should know better."

"Maybe a little. I mean, we never talked about how many kids we wanted. And the girls are older and in school. It'll be like starting over. And I'm really not looking forward to raising another child alone."

"So that's where all this is coming from." The puzzle pieces dropped into place. He didn't doubt her concern, and she'd made a good point, but it was only part of it. It wasn't fair that she was trying to make him feel guilty for doing all he could to provide for his family.

Of course, he missed her and the girls. Hated that they were growing up without him, but this was his career—the one he wanted. She'd known from almost day one that this was the path he'd chosen, and how important it was to him. But he couldn't deny the truth of what she said either. Most of their married life he'd been overseas somewhere, usually in a war zone, while she had all the responsibilities at home. But wasn't that what a military wife was supposed to do?

"No, that's not where 'this is coming from.' I know how important your career is but isn't your family just as important? You can still advance if you're here. Surely all these deployments have to count for something?"

"I'm sure they do."

"Will you at least think about it?"

"I don't know, maybe. Do I have a choice?"

"I can't believe you just said that. Maybe I should just give this baby to Lily like you suggested earlier? That would solve everything, right? No new baby, no reason to come home and be with your family."

Chloe stormed through the glass doors and into the suite without another word. What the hell? He didn't know what to think, they went from talking about his nightmares to changing his job, to a new baby. She was strung tighter than a violin and he didn't know how to diffuse the situation. He tried to remember what she was like during her last two pregnancies. Then he realized he wouldn't know. He'd barely been around and hadn't been home for either of the girl's births. Guilt kicked him in the stomach. She was pregnant with their child, and instead of celebrating they were fighting.

He needed a drink before he did anything else and not from the water bottled she'd given him earlier. This called for something a lot harder. He'd half expected to find her on the couch waiting to talk to him, but she was nowhere to be seen. Locating the mini-bar, he pulled out a couple of bottles of scotch and downed them straight from the bottle. Grabbing a couple more and a glass, he went back outside onto the patio. They needed time to cool off. If he talked to her now it would make everything worse. It was better to give her some space.

He was half tempted to call Alex and to tell him about the baby and all the other shit. He might have too if his phone hadn't been on the table next to the bed. Nope, he wasn't going in there yet.

This was some fucked up shit. Here he'd

done everything he could to make this a special weekend for her and this is how she appreciated his efforts. What the fuck? Not that he expected her to thank him but turning his nightmare into a reason to change his career plans sucked balls. Then throwing his words in his face. She had to know he was kidding when he said they should give one of their kids to Lily. She professed to know him, so again, what the fuck?

Lifting his glass in a toast to the cosmos, he took a long drink. The scotch burned a trail of fire to the pit of his stomach. At least, it took away the chill from the breeze brushing over his naked skin. He should have put on a t-shirt or something, the boxers weren't much cover. The weather in Florida was like night and day from the constant dry desert heat, but he sure as shit didn't miss it. He hated the sand and the freezing cold nights, but like he'd told Chloe it was his job. It was almost time for his evaluation, definitely not the time for a change, even if he'd had enough desert to last him a lifetime.

Another swig of scotch and the four bottles were history. He opened the next two and refilled his pity party in a glass. He loved Chloe, but damn she could be pig-headed. But it was part of what he loved about her. She'd never been a pushover and didn't fall for him because of his uniform like so many of the other girls. It was crazy how many girls just wanted to date him because of his uniform.

She'd made sacrifices, they both had, but he'd thought they were on the same page. But she sure as hell burst that bubble. The yawn caught him by surprise. Stretching out on the chaise, he took another drink. The sun was just peaking over the horizon, painting the sky with the deep purples and reds of pre-dawn. He really should go in and talk to her. Yup, he would, just as soon as he finished his drink.

∾

Chloe was spitting mad. If she'd been at home, she probably would have thrown something at Logan's head. Instead, she went inside, slammed the bedroom door, and threw herself onto the bed and cried. Then cried some more. She hated crying, despised it with a passion, but sometimes it was the only way to release the pent-up emotion and anger. Being pregnant didn't help the situation either.

Sure, she'd been the one to run off, but it

was that or say something she'd be sorry for later. They rarely fought. She couldn't remember the last time so maybe they were due. Too bad it had to be when they were alone in one of the most romantic places they'd ever been. Just thinking about it made her cry harder. Gut-wrenching sobs shook her entire body and soaked the pillow. Eventually, she cried herself to sleep, still hoping he'd come in and apologize.

The ringing phone woke her. Half asleep she reached for her cell before she realized it was the suite's phone.

Clearing her throat, she answered, "Hello?"

"Mrs. Mitchell?"

"Yes?"

"This is the front desk. I'm calling to confirm the reservation for the boat this morning."

Shit. She'd totally forgotten about their morning plans. She doubted Logan would want to go. She sure as hell didn't feel like being alone in a small boat with him at the moment. Speaking of 'him' where was he? He'd never come back to bed.

"Mrs. Mitchell?"

"Yes, sorry. I was thinking. Thank you for

checking with us, but I think we're going to have to cancel. I'm so sorry, and I'll pay any charge since it's last minute."

"Oh, it's no problem. Have a great day and if there is anything you need let us know."

"Thank you." Hanging up the phone, she made a mad dash for the bathroom. The girls called them the pee-pee dance, and it was one of the things about being pregnant she could have lived without. Now that she was wide awake, she took a shower trying to delay dealing with Logan as much as possible.

The collection of empty scotch bottles on the island in the kitchen didn't bode well. Sure enough, he was stretched out on the chaise and snoring loud enough to wake the dead. The only time he was that loud was when he'd had too much to drink. Seeing four more bottles sitting on the table next to him, told her all she needed to know.

Most of her anger dissipated while she was in the shower, but it was back with a vengeance. She couldn't believe he decided that the right choice was to drink himself into oblivion rather than talk to her. So much for a romantic weekend.

It didn't often happen, maybe three or four

times since she'd known him, but when he drank like that it usually took him most of the day to sleep it off. They should have spent the day having fun, so with or without him it's what she would do. No way was she going to sit there twiddling her thumbs waiting for him to get over it. But first she needed to eat. Even the sour scent of scotch didn't stop her stomach from growling. They hadn't eaten much yesterday, probably not the best thing for the baby either.

Leaving Logan to sleep off his alcohol-induced coma, she grabbed her purse, cell phone and one of the key cards. Making her way along the path they'd taken yesterday, she stopped by the main building to get something to eat and figure out a plan. Exploring the island sounded like a great idea, and while she was at it, maybe she'd figure out what to do next.

CHAPTER 10

It was Sunday morning and considering it was a semi-large resort, she was surprised there were so few people out and about. She'd read about the excellent meals served at the Thistle Lodge so that was her destination. It was too early to experience their Sunday brunch, but the waitress suggested the brioche French toast. It was delicious, maybe the best she'd ever had, and she couldn't thank the woman enough for the suggestion. After she finished, she stopped by the front desk to get some suggestions for her little exploration. Katie was at the desk again and recommended renting a bike from Billy's. She also gave her a couple of maps of spots to stop and explore, and get some shopping done.

"You have to go to Pinocchio's. Unless you don't like ice cream?"

"Are there any people who don't like ice cream?"

Katie laughed. "If there are they're a little crazy if you ask me. But it's to die for. They make everything themselves. It's worth every calorie."

"I will definitely check that out. Thanks."

Looking forward to some quiet time to sort through the thoughts running through her head, she had the valet get the car and drove into town. Armed with the map and directions, she meandered down the long entry road of the resort, enjoying the bright summer morning. It was supposed to be a fun weekend, and she planned to enjoy it even if it killed her. Depending on how things went with Logan later, it just might.

Chloe drove down West Gulf Drive until she reached the main road. Following the directions Katie had given her, she drove into town and turned onto Periwinkle. Most of the shopping she was interested in, and the bike rental place was located there. She pulled into the parking lot and surveyed the area. It looked like the town she'd visited with her parents when she was a child. Colorful stucco buildings, some with awnings, and an overall sleepy feel. It would have been fun to explore with Logan, but her temper flared just thinking about him back at the hotel. Shaking her head, she reminded herself she was there to enjoy herself, explore, and maybe pick up a few gifts for Lily and the girls. Thinking about Logan could wait until later.

Bailey's General Store was her first stop since she'd forgotten to bring a water bottle from the suite. It wouldn't hurt to pick up some snacks either. Eating regularly staved off her morning sickness and she was all for that. It was a cute store, everything anyone would need just smaller than the Publix Supermarket at home. Wandering up and down the aisles, she found the snack section and grabbed a couple of packages of nuts, two protein bars, and a couple bottles of water. Now she was all set for a day of exploring. After checking out the bikes at Billy's, she decided she'd rather walk than risk the chance of ending up on her ass. Chance? Who was she kidding? She hadn't been on a bike in over ten years. It was pretty much guaranteed she'd fall flat on her face. Everyone said that once you learned how to ride you never forgot, but she was convinced they were full of crap.

The island was beautiful and even though it was warm, there was a constant breeze. Enjoying the freedom of a day without a schedule, she took her time as she walked down Periwinkle Street and stopped to browse when something caught her eye. At home life was dictated by the girls' school schedule and after-school activities. She wondered how they were doing and decided to check in. Finally locating her phone in the bottomless pit she called a purse, she dialed her friend.

"Shouldn't you be doing something naughty instead of calling me?"

"Hi, Lily, nice to talk to you too." That was met by laughter and it lightened her heart a bit. It also made her realize that although she'd been enjoying the day she had a gray cloud hanging over her after last night's argument.

"How is the resort? Is it as beautiful as it looked online?"

"Oh yeah. It's gorgeous. I'll take plenty of pictures and show you when we get back."

"Good. Why are you calling? Shouldn't you be enjoying the beauty and your husband? Are you worried the girls took me out?"

It was Chloe's turn to laugh. It was a thought, but her girls knew better, especially with Logan at home. "Nah, I know you're all fine. You are fine, right?"

"Yes, worry wart. We're having a great time. Right girls?" A chorus of yeses followed her question and she could hear Bella asking if she could talk to her mommy. "Do you want to talk to them?"

"Sure."

"Coming right up. We'll see who grabs the phone first. Don't hang up when you're done with them. Okay?"

"I won't." There was a brief argument about who would talk to her first. Chloe smiled, their arguing didn't bother her this time, probably because it wasn't her issue to deal with. Poor Lily.

"Mommy. I miss you. Are you having fun? Where's Daddy? Are you swimming in the ocean? Did you get me something? When are you coming back?"

"Whoa, Girly. Too many questions all at once."

"I'm sorry, Mommy." She could hear Lexie complaining to Lily in the background. She really owed her big time.

"It's okay, Baby. Let me see if I remember them all. I miss you and Lexie too. I hope you're being good for Lily."

"We are."

"Are you sure?"

"I'm trying." Chloe grinned. She knew how that went.

"That's good. Make sure you try as hard as possible, okay?"

"I will."

"We are having lots of fun, it's very pretty here and I'm taking lots of pictures to show you when I get home. I haven't been swimming in the gulf yet, but I probably will later."

"Okay, when are you coming home."

"We'll be there when you get home from school on Tuesday. Remember? We talked about that."

"Oh yeah."

"I love you, Girly. I'll talk to you tomorrow. Can I talk to Lexie now?"

"Okay. Bye Mommy. I love you."

"Hi, Mom."

"Hey, Lex. Are you having fun with Lily?"

"Yeah, we went for ice cream last night and then we had a Harry Potter Marathon."

"I bet that was fun."

"Lily even let us stay up until Midnight." She could hear Lily reminding her that she wasn't supposed to tell. "Oh yeah. I wasn't supposed to tell you that." Chloe tried to hold back her laughter, she really did, but failed miserably.

"It's okay. It's the weekend and a special occasion."

"What are you going to do today?"

"We're going to the mall. Lily said we can each pick out one new outfit."

"That's really nice. Don't forget to say thank you."

"Mom. Geesh. I know."

"Okay then. I love you and I'll probably call tomorrow to see how you're doing."

"You don't have to. You're supposed to be having grown up time with daddy." Chloe knew exactly where that line had come from.

"We are, but it doesn't mean I don't have time to check on my girls."

"Okay. I love you too. Bye."

"I guess I should have remembered that kids can't keep anything secret," Lily said after she grabbed the phone from Lexie.

"Yup. You really should remember that. It's not the first time you've been burned."

"Nope, and I'll wager it won't be the last time either."

"I'm shocked, you haven't said a 'bad' word this entire conversation."

"Please, curse jar or not, your little kid is driving me out of my mind. Every time I say something I shouldn't she reminds me I should be putting money in the jar."

"Bella?"

"Who else? Although the other one laughs every time she does it."

"That's too funny."

"Easy for you to say. You're off in paradise with Mr. Hunk."

"Yeah, well I left Mr. Hunk passed out in a drunken stupor at the hotel. I'm exploring old Sanibel by myself."

"What the fuck? Oh shit." As soon as the word was out of her mouth, Chloe heard Bella's reprimand and giggled. "Do you see what I mean?"

"Yeah. Sorry. I'll have a talk with her when I get back."

"Wait. Let me get this straight. You're on your anniversary trip but you're sightseeing all alone?"

"Yup."

"What the h… heck is going on?"

"Shh, I don't want the girls to hear what we're talking about. They're smarter than you think and pick up what they hear like sponges."

"Girls, I'm going to make some more popcorn. Be right back. Okay, we're alone now, tell me everything."

"It was going really well at first. The resort is beautiful, everyone is friendly, and the room is gorgeous…"

"Got it, I want to hear about the shit that's going on with Logan."

Chloe sighed. She'd wanted to talk to Lily but dreaded it at the same time. But it was the only way to figure out if she was overreacting. Pregnancy hormones sucked donkey balls. "It started after Logan had a nightmare."

"Oh shit."

"Exactly. Apparently, he's had them for quite a while, probably close to a year. Remember when Sherm was killed? They started then."

"I remember. It was bad. Then after that Mac and Tag were hurt and the other guys…" Neither of them wanted to think about it.

"Yeah. I was happy when he opened up finally and explained what they were about. We talked about it, but then I made the mistake of mentioning that maybe he should think about not taking another tour and see about staying here."

"Fuck."

"Pretty much. It went over like a lead balloon. I should have known better. He was already sensitive from the dream."

"What did he do?"

"Oh wait, it gets worse. Guess who blurted out they were having another baby right then?"

"No. You didn't."

"Yup, I sure did. Talk about open mouth insert foot. I'd been so worried about telling him, what do I do? Share my big news at the worst possible moment."

"Oh Honey, I'm so sorry. I can just about picture that scene."

"You'd probably be right too. It blew up and I went to bed and cried myself to sleep. I guess he decided to tie one on because when I got up he was out cold on the balcony with a bunch of empty bottles from the mini-bar."

"You didn't wake him up?"

"Nope. I figured it would be better to let him sleep it off. I went for breakfast, which was excellent by the way. Then drove into town and I've been here ever since."

"But you're by yourself."

"It's not so bad. It's quiet, beautiful..." Even as she said the words her eyes filled with tears. This wasn't how she should be spending the weekend.

"I hear the tears in your voice. Chloe, you need to go back and talk to that man. Work it out. You need this weekend together. Don't let this ruin it."

"But..."

"Nope no freakin' buts. You'd tell me the same thing. You love each other, now go work it the fuck out."

"Ohhh bad word, really, really, bad word," Bella's voice carried over the phone and it was just the break in the tension that Chloe needed.

"The popcorn is almost ready. I'll be there in a minute or two. Your kids don't listen all that well, do they?"

"It depends. And you're right. We're both stupid. I'll finish my excursion and head back to the suite. Hopefully, he'll be up by then."

"Good."

"I'm kind of surprised he hasn't called."

"If he's still sleeping when you get back,

you need to wake his ass up. Pour some coffee down his throat and sit down and hash it out. Call me tomorrow and let me know how things went."

"I will. Thank you."

"What are friends for if not to kick each other in the ass when we go off the rails?"

"Ain't that the truth."

"I love you. Thank you again for everything."

"You're welcome, and I love you too. Oh my God, I just realized that the next time you go away I'll be watching three kids. Shit. Now get. I'll talk to you tomorrow."

"Okay. Bye, Brat."

Chloe felt a whole lot better after talking to the girls and Lily. She was right, of course. They needed to talk this through like adults. Checking the time on her phone, she was surprised it was after one. That made it more surprising she hadn't heard from Logan yet. He should have woken up by now. She hadn't missed any calls and there were no new text messages. Maybe he was still asleep or mad.

With a sigh, she stood up from the bench and continued down Periwinkle. There were a few more shops she wanted to visit before she headed back to the hotel. Yes, she was stalling, but another half hour or so wouldn't hurt anything. Since she hadn't heard from him yet, he was probably still sleeping. What was the point in hurrying back?

Snacking on some of the nuts and drinking one of the waters as she window-shopped, she found a cute little jewelry store. It was filled with locally-made items. Finding a beautiful sea glass bracelet that was perfect for Lily, Chloe was thrilled to find it. The polished sea glass beads were the muted greens and blues of the Gulf of Mexico and she'd love it. The girls were a little harder, but after looking through a few other stores she found cute stuffed sea turtles and bought two of the same ones to avoid any arguments. She'd learned that lesson the hard way. They'd always wanted what the other one had. Hopefully, they'd outgrow it soon.

After picking up a small gift for her mom, souvenir shopping was complete. After checking her phone for missed calls or a text, she was surprised that she hadn't heard from Logan. It was crazy that she'd been shopping and wandering around for over four hours. She couldn't remember the last time she'd done anything uninterrupted for more than a half hour, and it would be a long time before it happened again, that's for sure. Once this new little one was born her quiet time would drop to zero. Absentmindedly, she rubbed her little baby bump and smiled. A precious little life growing inside. The sweet scent of a newborn baby flooded her mind, and then the memory of her girls' first smiles. It was worth all the extra work, stretch marks, and sleepless nights to come.

On the way back to her car, she stopped at the ice cream shop Katie told her about. Pinocchio's was everything she'd described and more. Just picking a flavor was hard, so many she'd never heard of and would have liked to try. But after studying the menu, she finally settled on a two-flavor cup.

"Here you go, Hun. A caramel pecan praline and chocolate sand dollar cup."

"Wow, that's huge," Chloe said as she reached across the counter for the overflowing cup of ice cream. "Umm, why the elephant? Is it for first timers?"

The woman smiled. "Nope, it's a tradition here."

"It's a first time for me. I've never had an animal cracker on top of my ice cream."

"That's because you've never been in Pinocchio's. If it doesn't have the animal cracker you're not getting the real thing."

"Ahh, I get it. My daughters would go crazy in here. I'll have to bring them next time I come. Thank you, again."

"You're welcome. Enjoy."

The ice cream was delicious, and an excellent reason for delaying her return to the hotel. There was no way she'd be able to drive and eat the huge cup of frozen deliciousness. Instead, she sat at one of the wrought iron café tables in front of the shop and enjoyed every bit while she people-watched.

CHAPTER 11

The heat of the sun beating on his face woke Logan from his scotch-induced slumber. Disoriented, it took him a few minutes to realize he'd spent the rest of the night on the balcony. Craptastic. Chloe was going to be pissed. Then he snorted. Was going to be? Fuck. She'd been beyond that last night or actually it had been early morning if he remembered right. As he sat up, the world started spinning. He's just made a huge mistake. The swirling in his head and bile rising in his throat spelled imminent disaster. Sucking in deep breaths, he cradled his head in his hands and rested his elbows on his knees. Thankful no one was around, he focused on the sound of the ocean to get control of the roiling in his stomach.

As the sweats stopped, he was able to open his eyes and their argument filled his thoughts. It hadn't started out as an argument, and he wasn't sure how it had morphed from him sharing his nightmares to making him feel like he'd deserted his family. As if that hadn't been enough. For years she'd begged him to open up about things, to share so they could work it out together and then what happens when he does? She flips out and hits him with a real bombshell. A new baby. He'd never even considered that they'd have another one, not that he was upset about it. It was a baby—their baby.

Groaning, as his head throbbed, little flashes of lights dotted his vision. It was a sure sign a migraine was on the way. He definitely fucked it all up. There was no doubt it was all his fault, she didn't have to tell him—even though she would. This was all on him. He was always away, leaving her to raise their daughters on her own. It didn't matter that she'd agreed to this life when they'd gotten married. He'd never asked her again, never took into consideration the sacrifices she'd had to make for him. It had always been about his career advancement, ostensibly to make their lives better. But who the fuck was he kidding? He'd loved it, the thrill of not knowing what was next. Until this past year when it had started to change. So many friends over the years. But Sherm's death had really gotten to him. Then the IED took out Mac's Humvee and half his unit. It was the start of the nightmares and his doubts. What if it had been him? What memories would the girls have of him?

None of this was helping the throbbing in his head or the burning in his stomach. He needed to get his ass in gear. It was a bad sign that Chloe hadn't woken him yet, and from the location of the sun, it had to be near mid-afternoon. She was probably still pissed. How long had he been out there? It had probably been a pretty picture for housekeeping if they came by and saw him stretched out in his boxers. Son of a bitch.

The four empty scotch bottles lined up on the little table reminded him of his stupidity. Based on how shitty he felt, there were probably more empty bottles somewhere. That he couldn't remember how many more made him wince. Not good at all. He wasn't used to drinking hard alcohol, hell he rarely had a beer.

Bagram Air Force base was in a no drinking, no smoking area out of respect for the locals.

Plenty of the guys snuck cigs, but alcohol was confiscated when it was discovered. The last thing their superiors wanted was for them to disrespect the local religion. It was crazy since at least half of them made it their life's work to kill as many westerners as possible. Fuckin' jihad.

Time to quit stalling. Standing slowly, he hoped he wouldn't spew whatever was left in his stomach. Cautiously, he put one foot in front of the other, taking care not to move too much and trigger the migraine that was waiting to blow up in his head. Offering up a prayer that Chloe wouldn't yell when she saw him, he opened the glass doors and with a sigh went inside.

The cool air washed over his sun-heated body, raising goosebumps on his arms and naked chest and easing the pain in his head. It was quiet, too quiet. There was no sign of Chloe. As he searched the suite he also checked to see if she'd left him a note. Nothing. Not a damn thing. Maybe she'd sent a text, but he couldn't remember where the hell he'd left his phone. Fuck. This is what he got for drowning his sorrows in a bottle of scotch. Turning too quickly, he got dizzy and had to lean against the wall to settle his stomach. Asshole.

Taking one step at a time he made into the bedroom and returned to the scene of the crime —aka nightmare—that had triggered this disaster. Why couldn't he have gotten through a couple more nights without having the damn dream? He'd managed to hide them from everyone but Alex for the last year. So why now? When it caused more damage than he could have imagined.

At least he found his phone. Grabbing it from the bedside table, he swiped across the screen. Nothing. No missed calls or texts. But it verified that she was even more pissed than he realized. Finding him passed out on the balcony in a drunken stupor probably pushed her over the edge. He grimaced as he imagined the *lovely* picture. Stretched out on the chaise lounge, snoring, and probably drooling. It was going to take a lot of sucking up to fix this mess. For a moment he wondered if she'd been pissed off enough to go home, leaving him stuck there. But he knew better. She was too soft-hearted and would never do that no matter how mad. Oh, she was pissed—but vindictive? Never.

During their first year of marriage, he'd

learned that if he made a mistake the best thing to do was apologize, and he wasn't above groveling. No point in putting it off any longer, the sooner they talked about it, hopefully, the sooner they could move on and enjoy the time they had left on the island. Should he start with 'I love you?' She was probably too pissed for that. Better to start with an apology to gauge her response. Yup, he was a dumb chicken shit, but he wasn't stupid.

Hi, baby. I'm so sorry about last night. Where are you?

Running his hand over his face and feeling the scratchy day-old beard, he figured he could hop in the shower while he waited for her answer. With any luck, by the time he was done, she'd be back, and they could calmly talk it out. Clean, shaved, and smelling a whole lot better, he pulled on a pair of shorts and a polo shirt. There still was no sign of Chloe and she hadn't answered his text.

Now he was starting to get worried. They were in an unfamiliar place, he had no idea when she'd left or where she'd gone. She could have gone just about anywhere, but they'd never been to Sanibel Island before, so she'd probably stopped by the front desk for information. One of the keycards and her purse was gone so she'd probably taken the car somewhere. If she'd stayed on the resort property she wouldn't have taken her purse. Pulling his phone from his pocket, he checked again to makes sure he hadn't missed a call, and double check he had reception in the room, but he had all five bars. That meant she was either still pissed, her phone was dead, or she was hurt. Had something happened to her and or the baby? Fuck. She could have had an accident, or drowned in the gulf, all because he wasn't there when she needed him. Just like with Sherm. He was a fuckin' disaster, how could he have let this happen? Fear gripped his heart and twisted until he doubled over and ran to the bathroom losing his stomach contents.

Vomiting increased the pounding in his temples tenfold. The migraine was determined to show its ugly face, and he was just as determined to ignore it. After swallowing a couple of Advil and half a bottle of water, he shoved his phone in his pocket, grabbed the other keycard and went searching for his wife.

First stop was the main building. The woman who had checked him in was at the desk. Good. Maybe she'd remember them.

"Hi, I'm Logan Mitchell, do you remember my wife and I from yesterday?"

"Yes, of course, Lt. Mitchell."

"Great. I was wondering if you've seen Chloe today?"

"Did you misplace her?" She answered with a smile and wink. Normally, Logan would have laughed, but he was not in the mood for games. All he could picture was Chloe lying by the side of the road hurt or worse.

"I guess you could say that. Did you see her today?"

"Yes, she had breakfast and then stopped by to ask about sightseeing spots." Good, at least someone had spoken to her. She was still safe at breakfast time.

"Oh okay, so she went into town?"

"I think so. She didn't say where she was headed but when she asked about shopping I told her she could find just about everything she'd need on Periwinkle."

"Do you know if she took the car?"

"I think so. But you could check with the valet. Harry's been on all day, so he'd remember."

"Thank you, Katie. I appreciate your help."

"It's what we're here for. If you need anything, let me know."

Walking into the bright light, he cursed himself for leaving his sunglasses in the room. Debating on whether to go back and get them to ease his headache, he decided against it. His worry for Chloe won out. As soon as he stepped through the front doors, Harry the valet greeted him.

"Can I help you, Sir?"

"Actually, yes. Do you know if my wife took our car out?"

"What kind of car is it?" Shit, Logan, get your head out of your ass. It had to be the remnants of the alcohol, he was better than this.

"It's a twenty-ten dark blue Jeep Cherokee. Plate number X47RG2." He went over to his stand and looked through his notebook.

"Yup, the car was taken at ten-oh-six this morning."

"It hasn't come back yet?"

"No, Sir. At least not through here. Is there something else I can help you with?"

"That's it, thank you. Does the hotel have any transportation around the island?"

"There's a trolley that runs on a regular

schedule to different areas or you can call a taxi."

"Okay, thanks for your help."

"You're welcome."

Now what? Did he go into town and try to track her down? What were the odds he'd find her? At this point, she could have gone just about anywhere on the island. He'd never known her to spend this long shopping for anything.

Walking toward the parking lot, he hoped she'd show up before he had to decide on his next move. The path to the parking area was lined with bright pink oleanders. He should have been walking with Chloe, or wandering the beach and collecting seashells, or better yet, making love in that huge king-size bed in the suite. Instead, once again he'd fucked up big time. Maybe he should just retire, was he even fit to lead men or protect his family? Shaking off the self-doubt that had been his best friend for most of the last year, he focused on his next move.

It didn't leave many options at this point. Three that he could think of, the first was to keep calling and texting and hope she'd just show up even if she didn't answer him. The second was to take the trolley thing into town and hope she was still there or that someone would remember her and direct him in the right direction. The last would probably yield the most information but would also give him the biggest headache. The not knowing where she was and if she was okay was driving him crazy. He needed information and he needed it now, that left the third option.

Suck it up, buttercup. You brought this on yourself. Pulling his phone out of his pocket, he dialed Lily's number. Wincing, knowing he was in trouble before she answered, she would release a ton of shit on his head.

"How fucking stupid are you?"

"Uh, hi, Lily, nice to talk to you too."

"Don't 'hi Lily' me. What is it with you men? Are you all born without common sense?"

Oh yeah, she didn't disappoint him at all. But at least, he knew she'd spoken to Chloe. "Apparently not. I know I screwed up, believe me. I don't know how it got so out of control."

"I do. You're an asshole. How could you make her feel like you don't want the baby? What the fuck is wrong with you?"

More than just pissed off she was hurt. Alex

had told him how not being able to get pregnant was devastating for her. "I didn't, not exactly. I think she overreacted a bit…"

"Mother fucker, don't you even…"

"Listen, I'm sorry. Of course, I want the baby. It's ours there would never be any scenario where I would be anything else than thrilled."

"Well then maybe you should have led with that last night, huh? Asshole. She's been so worried about how you'd react."

"Did she tell you when she blurted it out? It's not all my fault…"

"Fuck…" In the background, he could hear his girls yelling at Lily about her cursing and it almost made him smile, almost. He still didn't know where Chloe was and if she was okay. "Do you see what you've done? Now I'm going to have to listen to your kids tell me how bad I am for the next hour."

"I'm sorry. I really am. Do you want me to talk to them?"

"No, you need to talk to Chloe. In fact, why are you calling me? Did something happen to her?"

"No, at least I don't think so."

"What the fuck does that mean? Yes, girls, I know. I'm sorry."

"It means she's not here. I haven't seen her since I woke up."

"Shit. When I talked to her she said she was going back to the suite to talk to you."

"When was that?"

"Uh, not sure, somewhere around twelve or one I think." It was after three.

"I guess she changed her mind, huh? I'm not going to lie. I'm worried."

"You should be, if you hadn't been such an asshole she'd be with you now."

"You think I don't know that?"

"Maybe she's just not answering you. Let me try calling her. Keep your panties on."

"Call me back."

"You'd better be prepared to do some major groveling."

"Just call Chloe, please. You can continue the torture later."

CHAPTER 12

Stashing her packages in the trunk, she got into the car and was fastening her seatbelt when her phone rang. Pulling it out of her purse, she was surprised it was Lily.

"Hey girl, what's up?"

"Where the fuck are you?" Lily whispered, probably so the girls wouldn't hear her.

"I was shopping and having ice cream. It's so beautiful here…"

"Weren't you going back to the hotel to talk to Logan?"

"Yeah, I am doing that now."

"Have you spoken to him yet?"

"No, why?"

"Because he called me half out of his mind with worry since he couldn't get a hold of you."

"Shit. When I checked my phone last he hadn't called or texted."

"Check it now."

Sure enough, there were four missed calls and a text message from him. "I see them now. Maybe I didn't hear them while I was walking around, and my phone was in my purse. I didn't deliberately not answer."

"Whether you did or not, you better call him before the guy has a heart attack. I gave him a hard time already, but I could tell he's really freaked out."

"Thanks. Can you do me a favor? Can you call him back and tell him that I'm on my way back to the hotel?"

"Okay. Any other message?"

"No, and ease up on him, he's probably beaten himself up enough already."

"Do I have to?"

"Yes. You do."

"Fine. You take all my fun away. Call me later and let me know how it went."

"I'll call you tomorrow. Go have some fun with the girls. Love you."

"Love you too."

There were two voicemails, both from Logan. Listening to them didn't tell her much about what he was thinking. When he'd woken up, had he thought about what they'd said last night?

After her day, she felt better about everything. Maybe she'd just needed some alone time to get her head together. But she didn't want to argue about it anymore, they needed to figure out what they were going to do going forward. She loved him, and she wasn't going anywhere no matter how pigheaded he might be. He was her husband, the girls' father, they were a family, and she had every intention of making sure it stayed that way.

As she turned into the entrance of the resort, a wave of nausea hit her hard. Saliva pooled in her mouth and she broke out in a sweat. Regretting eating all the ice cream, she prayed she'd be able to get back to the suite before she threw up. Dammit. She'd hoped all the morning sickness was over, but maybe it was stress related. This weekend hadn't turned out the way she'd expected, and she couldn't blame it all on Logan either. She'd begged him to open up to her about the nightmares and when he had, she turned it into a life discussion. It was the one she'd avoided having at other more appropriate times. Awesome, Chloe.

Another wave of queasiness made her pull over to the side of the road. After a few deep calming breaths and a drink of water, she closed her eyes and leaned against the headrest. It would be okay. They loved each other. They'd get through this like they had everything else over the years. It was just one stupid argument. Maybe not stupid, but ill-timed for sure. Taking another swig from the water bottle, she was about to put the car in drive when she felt it. A movement. Not a kick. But no doubt in her mind that it was the baby making their appearance known. "Okay, little one, what am I going to call you? Since I don't know if you're a boy or a girl, how about Sprout?"

As if answering her, there was another push, and tears filled her eyes. This baby, her family, that's what was important. Instead of fighting, they should be enjoying their time together. They needed to get over it. Checking to make sure there was no traffic, she pulled back onto the resort entrance road. A newfound sense of calm brought a smile to her face. Dropping her hand to her growing baby bump, she whispered, "Sprout, you're going to love our family. We're a little crazy, but you'll always be surrounded by lots of love. And just wait until you meet your sisters. Oh boy."

A strange feeling told her to go to the parking lot instead of using the valet. She'd learned a long time ago to trust her instincts and she wasn't about to second guess them now. Watching for the entrance to the lot closest to their building, she turned in and then parked in the first spot she found.

A familiar figure paced back and forth on the walkway in front of her with a phone held tightly to his ear. Was he waiting for her or was there some other reason he was there? She'd seen him pace while talking on the phone, but it usually involved work which seemed unlikely. Unless it had something to do with is meeting at the base? Was he still talking to Lily?

Watching Logan through the Jeep's window, she waited for him to realize she was there, but he was so intent on the call he didn't notice. She wasn't even sure he realized a car had pulled in next to where he was standing.

His body radiated tension, from the stiff line of his shoulders to the white knuckles wrapped around his phone. Something was wrong, terribly, horribly, wrong. Had something happened to the girls? Reaching for her phone, she checked for messages. Nothing except the one text he'd sent earlier.

So, it wasn't the girls. Lily would have called her first anyway. Then what? A chill slid down her spine as the nausea returned. Another swig of water eased some of the burning, but the expression on Logan's face was unmistakable. Something horrific had happened. She wasn't going to figure it out sitting in the car. Drinking some more water then taking a deep breath, she opened the door and climbed out of the car. As the door closed, he turned and met her eyes. Holding up a finger, he signaled for her to wait. She nodded in response. It was obvious he was speaking to a superior officer and it wasn't good news. Why call him when he was thousands of miles away from Afghanistan?

"Yes, sir. I understand. What about the colonel…"

Who was he talking to if not the colonel? The strain around his eyes and the hard set of his jaw broadcast his anger loud and clear but you'd never know it from his voice. It was calm, terse, and cold as ice. She'd only heard him speak like that one other time. It had been last summer at a BBQ they'd had. One of the younger guys acted up with the woman he'd brought. Logan let the guy have it. She hadn't known what his soldier persona was until then and it had scared the hell out of her. Now she was experiencing it for the second time.

"No, sir. I'll make sure I'm on the transport. Yes, sir. I'll take care of it." Hearing those words and seeing his tortured expression freaked her out. A loud buzz blocked his voice and the sunlight faded to gray. She had just enough time to reach for the car as she blacked out.

∼

It happened in slow motion, like a dream sequence in a movie. One minute Chloe was standing between him and the car trying to figure out who he was talking to and a split second later, he watched the color drain out of her face and she passed out. He dropped his phone and caught her just before she hit the pavement. After lifting her in his arms, he retrieved the phone to let the captain know what happened.

He was still talking, and he had to cut him off. "Sorry, Sir. But I'm going to have to get back to you. Chloe just passed out, and I'm standing in the middle of the parking lot."

"Okay, Logan. Get back to me as soon as you get home. I'll leave your orders at the base. Take care of your wife."

"Thank you, Sir."

Logan headed for the lobby hoping that being inside in the cool air would help revive her. He couldn't remember her fainting in all the time he'd known her. Was it the baby? Or something else?

As he crossed the marble floors of the lobby, Katie ran toward him.

"Oh no. What happened to Mrs. Mitchell?"

"I'm not sure. She fainted in the parking lot."

"Do you want me to call an ambulance?"

"No, I think she just needs to be inside in the cooler air. I'm sure she'll be fine in a moment." Chloe's eyes fluttered as she came to in his arms. He was never so relieved as when her beautiful blue eyes met his. "Would it be possible to get a cold drink for her?" he asked Katie.

"Of course, I'll be right back."

Thankfully the lobby was empty. The less commotion the better as he carried her to one of the couches and sat down with her in his arms. "Hi, Princess. Welcome back."

"What happened?"

"I don't know. I was hoping you'd tell me. One minute you were standing and the next you were out." As she grew more coherent, she must have realized they were inside the lobby and she struggled to sit up. "Easy, I don't think it's a good idea to make any sudden moves."

"I want to sit up."

Before he could answer, Katie was back with a bottle of water and some crackers. "I thought maybe a little food might help too. I can get something else if you'd prefer."

"This is great, thank you," Chloe said with a slight smile.

"If you need anything else let me know."

"Thank you, again," Logan answered, never taking his eyes off his wife. Slowly her color returned, but it only accentuated the black circles under her eyes. He'd put them there, he was sure of it. "Princess, drink some water." Her hand trembled as it brushed his to take the bottle.

"Thank you."

"How about a bite of a cracker. When was the last time you ate?"

"I'm not hungry."

"C'mon, just a bite or two. A plain cracker can't hurt. You used to eat them all the time when you were pregnant with Lexie."

"You remember that?" She asked as he helped her off his lap and onto the couch. She put the bottle on the table and dropped her head into her hands. She might not want to be in his lap, but he needed her close.

"Of course, I might not have been around a lot but when I am I do pay attention. You three are my life." Then he looked down and noticed the slightly rounded bump for the first time and gently rested his hand on it. "Did I just feel what I think I did?"

"The baby? Yup. Sprout's been quite active this afternoon."

"Sprout?"

"I didn't want to just say baby, or it, so Sprout."

He smiled. This is what made life worth living. Chloe was the love of his life and he needed to make sure she knew it. "I like it. Hey, Sprout, this is your dad." He swore the baby kicked again, but maybe it was wishful thinking. He needed some happy right now and feeling this new life filled him with a sense of hope. But it wouldn't ease the pain that was coming when he told Chloe the news.

"What's going on, Logan? I know you're stalling. I saw your face, heard your voice. Something terrible happened, right?"

"Yes. It's terrible."

"Just tell me, I know we have to leave. I heard something about a transport. I'd rather know now and not when we're stuck in the car for three hours."

Before he could answer, Katie was back with a tray of hot tea and cookies. He could have kissed her. He didn't know how to tell Chloe, and this gave him a few extra minutes to try to figure it out. She was going to lose it, and he was worried about her and the baby.

"I thought this might help a bit," Katie said as she placed the tray on the coffee table.

"Thank you, Katie. You're so sweet."

"I just hope you feel better, Mrs. Mitchell. You looked so pale."

"I am feeling a bit better and I'm sure these cookies will help. They look delicious."

"Oh good. Enjoy." With a smile for Chloe and a wink at Logan, Katie returned to her post at the front desk. He couldn't put it off anymore. He had to tell her something. She was right about him having to leave right away. The transport was leaving for Bagram AFB at oh-three-hundred. It was a three hour drive home and then he'd have another seven hours give or take to make sure everything was settled before getting on the plane.

As he looked into her worried blue eyes and saw her little laugh lines were much deeper than he'd remembered, it hit him like a punch in the gut. He didn't want to leave her, the girls, or his unborn child. The thought sent a cold shiver down his spine. He'd been doing it for years, it was what he'd wanted, when had it changed? He had to finish this tour, but then he'd be done, if they wouldn't station him stateside, he'd put in for retirement. He could find something to do. But now wasn't the time for this discussion either. There were more pressing matters to deal with, and he needed to make sure she was okay.

"Logan, enough. Stop stalling, I want to know what's going on."

He sighed. She didn't look like death warmed over anymore. That was a positive, but he was afraid she'd pass out again when she heard the news. "Since you're feeling better, let's head back to the room. I'll explain everything as we pack. You're right, I need to be on a transport asap. I'm so sorry. This isn't what I wanted for our weekend. I promise I'll make it up to you. But we need to leave now."

"Fine. The room it is, but don't think you can put me off one minute longer."

"I'd rather be in a secure area. And I want to make sure you're really okay first."

"I'm fine."

"Sure, you are. That's why you fainted. Have you ever done that before?" Logan asked as he took her hand to help her stand. It wasn't a long walk to the room and she should be fine, but he wasn't letting go. It was as much for him as it was for her.

She didn't answer right away, it seemed that it was her turn to stall. He could see the wheels turning in her mind as she tried to come up with something he'd believe. Her lips turned down. "No, I haven't."

"See. So, something isn't right. I'm worried about you, Princess. You scared the ever living shit out of me."

She blinked, and tears glistened in her eyes. He didn't wanted to upset her, but apparently, it was what he did best. "Please don't be upset, Sweetheart. I'm worried about you, you're my wife, my heart. Without you, I have nothing to live for."

More tears, and this time one escaped. Her tears tore at his heart. Before it could slide down her cheek, he caught it with his finger. Staring at the little glistening teardrop almost broke him. "We're going to be okay, right? I'm sorry about last night. Please say we're alright."

She nodded. "Yes. Of course, we are. You're my world, Logan. You and the girls…" She looked down and patted her stomach. "And Sprout. But now maybe you can understand a little of how I feel while you're away."

He knew exactly what she meant, but right now there wasn't a damn thing he could do about it.

CHAPTER 13

Walking hand in hand they were silent on the way to the suite. Every step increased his dread for the conversation they were about to have. He made a silent promise that he'd bring her back and they'd have their romantic weekend. It was a promise he'd keep no matter what, even if he had to save for a whole year to afford it.

After closing the door to the suite, he took her into his arms and kissed her, hoping she'd feel everything he was. The days, weeks, and months ahead were going to be brutal, now more than ever, and these stolen moments would have to hold him over until he returned. He hadn't planned on making love to her, just to pack and hit the road, but as they say the best-laid plans.

Lifting her into his arms he carried her into the bedroom, gently laid her on the bed and stripped out of his clothes. Starting with her eyelids, he kissed his way over her face, the tip of her nose, each of her cheeks and finally took her mouth in an almost frantic kiss. Desperation drove him, and she must have felt it too.

Pushing him onto his back, she pulled off her clothing, tossing everything onto the floor, and straddled him. Neither of them spoke, no words were needed, as always, they had that connection—two halves of their whole. She kissed down his chest, nibbled on his nipples before moving to his belly and lower. Groaning, he tried to hold still. To let her have her way with him. But he was filled with a desperate need to possess her, and when her hot mouth slid over his cock, he almost lost it.

"Oh, Princess. I can't. I need to be inside you," he moaned as he lifted her and placed her on her back on the bed. Pushing her legs open with his knee, he balanced on his forearms and his muscles clenched as he tried to maintain control. "I love you, Chloe." As soon as the words left his lips he buried himself deep inside her. Shaking with need, he forced himself to hold still to let her adjust to him before finding the rhythm they'd learned over the years. Taking it slow wasn't an option and as soon as her muscles tightened around his cock, he sped up until she quaked with the force of her orgasm. It pushed him over the edge and he collapsed, rolling to the side at the last minute worried he'd crush her and the baby.

Several moments later he finally caught his breath and rolled to his side to memorize every freckle, fine line, and the expression in her eyes. Wanting to hold her in his arms and cuddle for hours, reality flooded back with a vengeance. He'd stalled long enough, no matter how much he wanted to make love to her all night long and forget the rest of the world it wasn't possible. They needed to go, as it was they'd be cutting it close for him to make that transport. They had a long drive, and then he had to face the girls—and Lily. He wasn't sure which would be worse.

"I'm afraid we have to get going. I have to catch that transport."

"I know. But we're alone now, no one can hear whatever classified thing it is you have to tell me. What is it? What is so horrible you don't want to tell me?"

"There was an incident at the base. It's why I have to head back tonight."

"MacDill?"

"No, Bagram. I don't know all the details, and most of what I know I can't tell you, as usual. But there were a lot of injuries and damage. The captain needs me back." Yes, he was trying to lessen the blow, and no he couldn't tell her everything. But Captain Durand said it was a shitstorm of major proportions. For him to talk like that, Logan knew things were worse than he could imagine. Considering all the shit he'd seen over the years that was saying something. The captain told him more than fifty soldiers were either injured or dead, and then there was Alex.

As if just thinking his name triggered the universe, Chloe's phone rang. Logan knew without seeing the screen that it was Lily. She'd probably just been notified. His stomach clenched, and acid rose up to burn his throat. He should have told her. Once again, he'd fucked up.

Chloe looked at him and then the phone. As if she could read his mind, her eyes filled with tears. "Oh no! Lily…" She answered the phone and the horror on her face told him all he needed to know. The captain hadn't had a lot of information about Alex or any of the wounded, it had been too soon. But he'd gotten the call over two hours ago. He could bet that they had an update on Alex's condition before they called Lily. He hated that his best friend had gone through this without him. But at the same time, he dreaded that it could have been Chloe getting the call instead of Lily, and it made him feel like a total asshole.

Tears slid down Chloe's cheeks as she listened to her best friend. Logan couldn't watch the torment on his wife's face, and he gathered their belongings and packed their bags. Eventually, she went into the other room after giving him a look that would have killed a lesser man. He understood her anger, but he'd only wanted to shield her for as long as possible. He was the protector, always had been, always would be, until he met his end.

After checking all the drawers and closet one more time, he carried the bags out to the living room. Chloe was sitting on the couch and staring off into space as silent tears slid down her face. Dropping the bags on the floor, he lifted her into his arms and sat down with her on his lap.

She buried her head in his chest and cried, heart-wrenching sobs that racked her body. Listening to her, holding her, his eyes misted. He wasn't ready to lose Alex. They'd been through so much together. Then he remembered that the girls were staying with Lily.

As if Chloe felt his thoughts, she looked up at him with red-rimmed eyes and flushed cheeks. "I called Mom, she's running over to get Lily and the girls and bring them back to our house. I didn't think Lily should be alone, and I didn't want her to have to deal with the girls until we got back."

"Good call. I'm sorry I didn't tell you about Alex. I didn't want to believe it myself. How is Lily, did she have any updates?"

"Just that he's been severely injured, and he's in surgery."

"Fuck. Not much more than I was told. I was hoping they'd have more information for her. I know at least twenty are dead, and about thirty others are wounded. I should have been there."

"You couldn't have stopped it from happening, you know that, right? And then I'd have gotten a call too. It's selfish of me, but I'm glad you weren't there. And I already feel guilty for thinking it, especially since my best friend may lose her husband."

Logan nodded. This was the harsh reality of war. He and Alex had been lucky, only sustaining minor injuries over the course of their careers. But it looked like Alex's luck might have run out.

CHAPTER 14

The trip home was quiet. They were lost in thought and worried about their friends. The romantic weekend hadn't gone at all the way they'd hoped, but the news from Afghanistan was devastating. Chloe's heart was broken for Lily and Alex. But she had to focus on Lily, to be the strength she'd need to lean on while they figured out how badly Alex was injured and what it would mean going forward. She'd been there for Chloe more times than she could remember and now it was time for her to step up and be the strong one.

When they were about an hour away from home, Chloe called to speak to the girls and her mom. They'd been scared when Lily started crying and thought they'd caused it. Thank goodness her mom was able to drive over to bring them back to their house and get them calmed down. She hated having to explain about their Uncle Alex over the phone, but there wasn't much she could do about that. Hopefully, they were too young to truly understand what was going on. After making sure they were okay she said goodnight and spoke to her mom.

"They seem to be doing okay," Margie Simon, said as she took the phone from her granddaughters.

"Yeah, they do. I really appreciate you doing this, Mom."

"Please, I'm your mother. I'm just glad I was home when you called. I was out on Harold's boat earlier and I wouldn't have had reception."

"I guess we got lucky. Bella will probably have a bad nightmare tonight. When anything upsets her during the day that's what happens. Can you listen extra in case she does?"

"Do you forget I was your mother? I do know how to take care of children. Stop worrying. Focus on Lily. She was a total wreck when I got there."

"I know. Or I should say I figured. When I

spoke to her she didn't even sound like herself."

"She's in shock and I don't think anything is sinking in right now. I tried to get her to come back with me and the girls, but she refused."

"Damn. I didn't want her to be alone."

"Me either. That poor girl needs to be around people who love her right now."

"After we get home I'll head over there. If I have to I'll make Logan carry her to our place."

"Sounds good. I'll make up the spare room for her, I can sleep on the couch."

"You can sleep in our bed. Logan's leaving, and I don't think I'll be sleeping tonight."

"Are you okay, Honey? You sound fine, but I know you."

"As good as can be. But I need to be strong for Lily. It's what I'm going to focus on."

"Good. Focus and positive thinking."

"Okay, Mom. I'm gonna hang up and try to get Lily. We'll see you in about an hour."

"Bye. Love you."

"Love you."

After disconnecting from her mom, she dialed Lily. Three times she tried but each time it just want to voicemail. She couldn't wait to get home to check on her. Being alone in that house was the worst thing she could imagine for her. Giving up on her answering, she shoved the phone in her purse and stared out the window at the passing cars. Her children were safe, her husband was safe for now, so all of her energy would go to helping her best friend deal with whatever was coming.

"How are the girls?" Logan's voice startled her, she'd been so deep in thought.

"They seem fine. But Bella tends to have nightmares when upsetting things happen during the day. Mom will listen for her though."

"Good. And Lily? Your mom couldn't get her to come to our house?"

"Nope. She's still at home."

"We'll stop by there after we check in at home. I still have to go by the base."

"How about you drop me off at Lily's on your way to the base. Take care of what you need to, and then swing back by her house."

"Are you sure?"

"Yup. It's okay, really. It'll probably be better if you're not there. I'm not sure how she'll react."

"Good point." Logan flashed her a quick smile, then returned his focus to the road. As she stared at his profile, she worried about what he'd be going back to. Would she be the next one to get a phone call? Or worse? The dreaded car pulling up in front of the house. Blinking her tears away, she put her hand over his where it gripped the steering wheel.

"Are you okay, Princess?"

"Yes, just worried about you."

"I'll be fine, don't worry. I have to be." Yes, he did, but how many other men and women had thought the same thing? How many were convinced they'd go back home when their tour was over, and how many had returned injured or worse in flag-draped caskets?

But thinking like this wouldn't help any of them. This danger wasn't new, but it sure as hell hit closer to home this time. Their men weren't invincible no matter how much they wished they were. Just thinking about him getting on that transport made her want to throw up. But as he'd said earlier, they had no choice. All she could do was pray he'd make it back home as soon as possible.

It was a bit after eight by the time they pulled into their driveway. Chloe's first instinct was to run inside and hold her daughters. Instead, she helped Logan carry in their luggage, hugged her mom, and then went quietly upstairs to check on her sleeping children. They had school in the morning, and as much as her world had been turned upside down, theirs meant they had to get up in the morning and get ready. That was the only thing she knew for sure, the rest of her reality had taken a left turn somewhere.

A half hour later they were back in the car. Logan needed to make sure his orders hadn't changed, and she needed to do whatever it took to get Lily to their house. Chloe had tried calling her at least seven times, and she hadn't answered once, which only worried her more. Lily put up a tough front, but Chloe knew how fragile she really was, and this could be enough to break her.

Logan pulled into Lily's driveway and stopped. "Are you sure you don't want me to come in?"

"No, it's okay. I'll be fine. You have things to do. She's probably just doesn't want to talk to anyone."

"I don't know, that's not the Lily I know. And you're practically her sister. Wouldn't she want to talk to you?"

"In her shoes, I'd probably be the same

way." He nodded, not wanting to think about that option any more than she did. "Anyway, go do your stuff. I'll call if I need you."

"Okay, Princess." As she started to get out of the car, he grabbed her arm and pulled her to him for a quick kiss. "Give Lily a hug from me."

"I will." After waving goodbye, she walked up the rest of the driveway to the front door. The house was dark, the sun hadn't been down too long, but it was strange not to see any lights on when Lily was home. Knocking but getting no answer, she tried the door. It had to be the one time Lily locked her door. They'd traded keys years ago, so even the locked door couldn't keep her out. Digging the key out of her purse, she unlocked the door and let herself in. The house was too quiet, creepy, like it knew there was something wrong and was sad.

"Lily?" No answer. A quick check of the downstairs showed no sign of her. The only light was from the TV which was paused on Frozen. Ironic really because her house looked frozen in time with the girls' drinks and a bowl of popcorn still on the coffee table like they'd just gotten up a moment ago. Turning on the lights, she picked up the dishes and carried them into the kitchen. The utter silence filled her with dread. She prayed that Lily hadn't done anything stupid. She probably should have run upstairs as soon as she'd gone inside, but she wasn't ready for the possibility of something horrific waiting for her upstairs. But she couldn't put it off any longer, and as she made her way upstairs she heard the bed creak. "Thank God," she whispered and knocked on the master bedroom door before going in.

Lying on the bed, curled around a huge stuffed teddy bear, Lily's body shook with soundless tears. Alex had brought it home with him at Christmas. Now she clung to it like it was a lifeline. Chloe fought back her tears, she needed to be strong. Lily didn't have any family besides them and Alex.

"Lily, honey, I'm here." Sitting on the edge of the bed, she pulled her friend into her arms, rocking as Lily cried. "Have you gotten any updates on Alex?"

"Not yet. I'm okay."

"No, you're not, and you don't have to be. I'm not either. I think you need to stay with us at least until we know more. It's not good for you to be here alone."

"I can't leave. What if Alex comes home?" Chloe sucked in a breath. What? Alex wouldn't be coming home any time soon. Not if he was in surgery three hours ago. It had to be shock. It wasn't rational. But would she be any better if she were in Lily's shoes?

"He won't be home tonight. He's in surgery, right? That's what you told me."

"But I have to wait for him. He might show up." Yup, definitely shock and denial, later would be anger and more tears. It was what they'd warned them about at their wives' meetings. There was no way she was leaving her there alone, even if she had to call Logan to come and carry her out. Or she'd stay there and take care of her.

"I promise, Lily. He won't be home tonight. He has your number. If he needs you he'll call. We'll make sure to keep the phone connected to the charger, so the battery won't die. Okay?"

"I need to see him," Lily said, her voice hoarse from crying.

"You will. You have to wait until he's in Germany. I'm sure they'll fly you there."

"Okay."

"Will you come back to my house?"

"I guess."

Throwing a few things into an overnight bag, Chloe was relieved that Lily agreed. Once she had her bag ready, she hugged her again. "All ready, let's get going. We'll take your car then you'll have it tomorrow. Sound good?"

"I guess so." With Chloe's help, she got up while still clutching the large teddy bear like it was a matter of life and death. She didn't blame her, it was the last thing Alex had given her and right now it was the closest thing to holding him.

~

Logan pulled into the parking lot at Fitzsimmons Air Force Base and shut off the car. It was the first time he let himself think about Alex. He'd been focusing on Chloe, the girls, and Lily. Dealing with the issues was his standard reaction in any kind of an emergency. But now, knowing everything else was handled, he thought about Alex. He didn't know much more than he'd told Chloe. There had been a truck bomb. How they'd gotten through gate security he had no idea. The force of the explosion rocked the base and took out most of the windows. The captain didn't even have a full accounting of the casualties when they'd spoken.

He should have been on base and not in Florida. If he hadn't been stateside for the meeting at MacDill, maybe he could have stopped it, or at least saved some of them. It was like Sherm all over again. He failed his men, and this time he'd failed his best friend too. Engrossed in his thoughts, he didn't even realize someone had approached the car until there was a knock on the window. "Great, lieutenant, way to get yourself killed."

It was the colonel, why he was standing next to Logan's car he had no idea. But it couldn't have been good. The colonel was an impatient man. No good could come of making him wait.

"Situational awareness is imperative, lieutenant."

"Sir," Logan replied as he got out of his car and saluted.

"At ease, soldier. Come to my office. I have a pouch you need to deliver to the base commander. The latest briefings just came in and I'll bring you up to speed."

"Yes, sir. Thank you," Logan said as he trailed behind the man his captain called a pompous bastard. Following the colonel to his office, he updated Logan with what he was cleared to know, which wasn't as much as he wanted to hear. Somehow one of the transport trucks had a bomb hidden in the engine at some point during operations, and once it was inside the barricades it was remotely detonated. They were doing search and rescue but the numbers the colonel had were fifty wounded, twenty-seven dead, and five missing. They were hoping they'd find the missing still alive as they sifted through the rubble. There was much still unknown.

It was a bold move, getting a bomb on a transport truck considering how often they were checked. It was also the first time it had happened at Bagram, but they should have been better prepared. Security measures would need to be re-examined and different options put in place. They'd thought they were safe once they'd returned to base, now they knew differently. That it took an incident of this magnitude was devastating. Now reinforcements were being sent back with him. Ironically, it had been one of the reasons he'd been stateside in the first place. It was going to be a long plane ride while wondering what he was going to be walking into.

Finishing up with the colonel, he verified his

orders and signed for the pouch he had to deliver to the Bagram Base Commander. Walking out to his car, he climbed in and headed home filled with dread about saying goodbye to his family and what he'd find when he got to Afghanistan. He didn't want to leave. Not that he'd ever wanted to be away, but it was his job. Until now. How horrible that it took Alex's being wounded to see what Chloe had been saying all weekend. Life was short, way too short. He'd missed so much of his daughters' lives. Did he want to miss the new baby's as well?

Arriving at the house, he was relieved to see Lily's car in the driveway. The last thing she needed was to be alone, and thankfully Chloe had been successful in getting her out of her house. At least, he hoped that's what it meant. As he opened the kitchen door, he caught a whiff of coffee beans. Chloe was making coffee, of course. It's what she did when she was worried, it probably hadn't even occurred to her that she couldn't drink it. When she saw him, she rushed into his arms and held him like her life depended on it. He tilted her chin up with his finger and kissed her, tasting the salt of her tears.

"Did find get more information? Do you still have to go back tonight?"

"Not really. It's a fuckin mess is what it is. A truck bomb went off inside the base, they're still not sure how it got through security. And yeah, I'm leaving tonight."

"What about Alex? Any news?"

"No. I wasn't able to reach the captain and the colonel either didn't have any specific information or he wasn't sharing it. I promise if I find out anything I'll let you know. But with protocol, they'll probably let Lily know first."

Chloe nodded. They knew all about protocol. All the wives were given packets of information when their husbands deployed the first time.

"How is she?"

"Not good. I had a hell of a time getting her to come with me. She kept insisting he was coming home and she had to wait for him."

"Shit. Where is she?"

"In the spare room. I told Mom she could have our bed. I don't think I'll be sleeping much."

"I'll check on her when I go upstairs to pack."

"How are you? How much time do we have?"

"About two hours. How are you holding up?" He couldn't answer the question about how he was, he didn't know. He was in react mode, but he wasn't looking forward to the trip. There would be way too much time to think.

"I have to be strong for Lily. I wish I knew what to do to help her. I'd be worse if it had been you, and just thinking about that terrifies me."

Logan nodded, he didn't want to think about it either. He'd thought Sherm's death hit him hard, but this was much worse. It was tearing him up. He didn't want to leave his family but the desire to go back and catch the people responsible was equally strong. So instead of dwelling on it, he poured a cup of coffee and went upstairs to repack his duty bag.

∽

The fifteen-minute drive to the airfield was both too long and too short. Every mile driven was one step closer to having to say goodbye to Logan. It was never easy, but this time it was so much worse. She'd left everyone sleeping at home, even Lily seemed to be sleeping finally. All her tears had worn her out, and the Tylenol PM she'd slipped into her coffee had probably helped.

It took every ounce of Chloe's strength to not plead with Logan to stay. To miss the transport. But it would have been pointless. It was his job. His men were injured, and she didn't have to ask to know he felt responsible. Nothing would convince him that he couldn't have done something to prevent it. He wasn't Superman. So instead, she took a deep breath and pasted a smile on her face. He'd be able to see through it, but she didn't want his last vision to be her in tears with snot dripping from her nose. Nope, she'd get through this, say goodbye, and then lose it after he was out of sight.

As they got out of the car, Chloe was surprised to see so many others waiting to get on the plane. Logan grabbed his bag from the back seat and came around to her side of the car. Taking her into his arms, he held her close for a moment and kissed her. He stared into her eyes, and she hoped he could see all the things she couldn't say.

"I didn't know so many others were going."

"Yeah, we need reinforcements." His expression grim as he looked at the others.

"I hate this."

"I know, believe me, and I'm sorry. But…" Instead of finishing the sentence pulled her closer and took her mouth in a fierce kiss that she felt down to her toes. She held on hoping to steal a few extra minutes with him. But as always, the kiss was over too fast, and he released her too soon. "It's time, Princess."

"I know. Logan, I love you. Please, please be safe and come back to us."

"I promise you that I will walk through that squeaky kitchen door and take you in my arms and kiss you like there's no tomorrow. And while I'm gone you'll be here." He took her hand and placed it over his heart.

With one last kiss, he smiled and walked away. As he disappeared into the darkness of the plane, she prayed. "Please God, bring him home safe and sound so this baby will know his father."

CHAPTER 15

Chloe walked in the door and was surprised to find Lily awake and sitting on the couch. It wasn't until she got closer that she realized she had her phone to her ear. Grabbing a couple of glasses of water from the kitchen, she quietly sat next to her and put the water on the table. Lily's eyes were red-rimmed and swollen, fresh tears still on her cheeks. This had been their worst nightmare with each deployment, and until now they'd been lucky. But it looked like that luck had run out. Now she felt guilty that her husband was okay while Lily's was God knows where fighting for his life.

"Yes, I understand. Okay. When? Yes. I'll be there. Thank you." Disconnecting the call, Lily calmly put the phone on the table and picked up the glass of water. It was strange to see her movements so deliberate, but it was probably the only thing holding her friend together.

"News about Alex?"

"Yup. He's out of surgery, but all they did was stabilize him. He'll need at least one more tomorrow when he gets to Germany."

"But he's stable enough to travel, right? That's really good news."

Lily nodded as tears slid down her face. "They said they're not sure he'll walk again. That he has a lot of shrapnel embedded near his spine. They were afraid to try to get it all out of there."

Chloe hugged her tight. She had no words that would help, they sounded lame when she thought about them. Alex was strong, he'd pull through, they'd learn to deal with it if he couldn't walk. It was the crap everyone said, and it didn't do a damn bit of good. They all knew how the spiel went.

"Honey, I'm not going to tell you it will be okay, because we don't know. But I'm here for you. If you want to scream, throw things, or just cry and rant. Whatever you need."

"I know. I appreciate it more than you know.

They're flying me to Germany tomorrow. There are three of us going. Karen, Angie, and Lori's husbands were wounded too."

"Damn. Logan said twenty-seven were killed. I haven't seen any official vehicles yet. Maybe they weren't from our base."

"Or they're waiting until morning. I didn't see anything on the news either."

The fact that Lily hadn't cursed once in the whole conversation worried Chloe more than anything else. The F-bomb was part of her normal vocabulary. "I wish I could go with you."

"I do too, but I'm glad you're not. It's bad enough that the others are going. I wouldn't wish this on anyone. And before you go there, don't you dare feel bad because Logan wasn't there. It's the job they chose, we knew this could happen."

"When did you start reading minds?"

"Apparently, it's a trick I just picked up," Lily said with a wry laugh. But it was a laugh and a small sign that her friend was still in there somewhere.

"What time do you leave?"

"They're sending a car for us around ten."

"Oh okay, I was going to ask if you needed me to drive you."

"They've got us covered. I should probably go home and pack."

"I think you can wait until morning. The girls have school, so we'll be up bright and early."

"I think I scared the shit out of them."

"Nah, they're fine. My mom said she got them settled down pretty quick. By the time we got home they were out cold."

"I wish this was a nightmare. I want to wake up and have our life back."

"I know, sweetie. I wish I could make it go away."

"Where's Logan?"

"He had to go back." A shiver of fear slid down Chloe's spine as she said the words. He would be okay, he promised.

"I wonder if he'll get to see Alex." Good question.

"It would be great if he could. He's devastated he wasn't there for Alex and the rest of the guys."

"Alex would be too." Pulling the afghan from the back of the couch, she wrapped it around Lily hoping it would help alleviate her shivering.

"Hey how about I make some hot cocoa?"

"That sounds good. But can you spike mine?"

"Probably not a great idea. I might have slipped you a sleeping pill earlier when I gave you that cup of coffee."

"Really? That's pretty devious for you. I'm impressed."

"I know, right? I guess you've finally rubbed off on me and I've grown a pair of balls." Lily snorted which made Chloe laugh until they were both laughing so hard they were holding their bellies. When they finally got a hold of themselves, they had tears running down their faces.

"What the heck is going on down here? Do realize it's almost five a.m.? You sound like a couple of chickens who escaped the hen house," Margie said as she stood yawning in the living room doorway.

"Sorry if we woke you, Mom."

"It's okay. It was kind of nice. Like the old days when you'd stay up all night plotting and laughing."

"Well, shit. Did we keep you up then too, Margie?"

"Yup, but it was okay. There's something about hearing you two in cahoots that fills my heart with happiness." Lily got up from the couch and hugged Chloe's mom.

"I hope you know that you've always been like a mom to me." Margie met Chloe's eyes over Lily's head and silently asked if things were okay. Chloe shrugged, she didn't want to take away Lily's few moments of happiness by talking about Alex.

"I'm going to whip up some hot cocoa. Do you want one, Mom?"

"Sounds great. But how about I make it while you two keep chatting."

"You don't have to…"

"Relax. I think I can handle it," Margie said with a chuckle as she walked away.

"She thinks of you like a daughter too, you know."

"Since I spent so much time in your house, I'd hope so. Either that or she was a really good actress." Thinking about the church talent show and her mom's performance started them laughing all over again. Father Gallagher had even made her promise to never participate again. Margie had been quite upset until she saw a video, and she'd forbidden them from ever talking about it.

"Crap we better be quiet, if we woke up Mom the girls are next. And we definitely don't want to deal with them on so little sleep."

"No shit. That fucking curse jar would be under my nose so fast my head would spin."

Chloe nodded and giggled. Bella was a piece of work with that jar, which was almost half full. Not sure it deterred any of them from their potty mouth's, but they'd be taking a trip sooner than later at the rate they were going.

It wasn't long before Margie was back with the mugs of hot cocoa and a box of Girl Scout cookies. How she'd found her stash, Chloe had no idea. They tried to keep the conversation light, lots of reminiscing. It was going well until Lily's phone rang. She took a deep breath before answering. Chloe's heart was in her mouth, so worried that he'd taken a turn for the worse.

"This is Lily Barrett." The color drained out of Lily's face and Chloe was thinking the worst until she spoke again.

"Alex? My fucking God. Are you okay? Where are you?"

Chloe was dying to know what he was saying, but she'd have to wait. The beautiful smile on her bestie's face was enough for now. She elbowed her mom to get her attention since they'd been staring at Lily. "Let's go in the other room and give them some privacy," Chloe whispered.

While waiting for Lily, Chloe shared what she knew about Alex with Margie while she washed the dishes. She'd swear the sink sprouted dishes on its own. No matter how often she did them there were always more waiting.

"I'm glad he called. To hear his voice has to be a huge relief," Margie said, as she dried and put away the dishes.

"Me too. Knowing he was able to call hopefully means it's not as bad as we thought."

"It sort of is and sort of isn't," Lily added. Neither of them heard her come into the kitchen. "They're getting him ready for the trip to Germany. They let him call before sedating him for the flight. He sounded pretty good, mostly pissed off. Standard Alex, right?"

Chloe smiled gently at her friend but wondered how much of his attitude was an act to reassure his wife. She knew Alex well enough to know he wouldn't be above doing that. He might relish giving everyone a hard time, but no one doubted how much he loved Lily.

"Yes, it is. I'd take that as a great sign."

"I need to believe that it is. I told him that I'd be there sometime tomorrow."

"Good. It'll be okay, you'll see," Margie said as she hugged Lily. "And now I'm going to go upstairs and shower before the little hellions wake up and demand breakfast. I promised I'd make blueberry pancakes."

"Oh boy, they played you. Didn't they?"

"Yup, they got me good. But it's okay. A good breakfast before school is good for them."

"Thanks again, Mom." Margie smiled and waved off her daughter's comment and left the two friends to talk.

"Do you really think it'll be okay?"

"Yes, I do. Alex is a fighter. He's not going to give up. But I'm not saying it's going to be easy either."

"Yeah, I'm already anticipating that. He can't stand being sick with the flu. I can't imagine if he's stuck in the wheelchair."

"Me either, but hopefully once he's healed he won't be."

"I hope you're right. Not that I care if he never walks again as long as he stays alive. He's the love of my life. I can't imagine living without him."

"I know, Honey. But like I said last night, no matter what, we're here for you. Me and Logan. You don't have to do any of this alone."

"That means a lot."

"It would never be any other way. Got it?"

"Yup. I think I'm going to go home now."

"Why don't you stay for breakfast?"

"Nah, I need to pack and get my head together. I asked Alex about the other men. Karen's husband is still unconscious, Lori and Angie's husbands took some shrapnel and have some burns."

"Logan said over fifty were wounded."

"Fuck. That many? I guess the others weren't stationed here. Alex just mentioned Ben, Tyler, and Mark."

"When Mac's Humvee hit the IED I thought that was bad. And now this. Doesn't it seem like things are picking up over there?" Chloe said as she gave her friend a hug on the way to the front door.

"Yeah. It does. I'm so sorry Logan had to go

back. At least, Alex won't be going back now. If there's a silver lining that's it."

Chloe was relieved that she was over the initial shock and trying to think positive. Even though she was traveling with the other wives, she still worried about Lily. She never did well in new environments, but she'd only be a phone call away.

∼

Chloe hadn't heard from Logan, and it had been almost a day since Lily had left to be with Alex. To say she felt lost was an understatement. At least she had the girls to take care of, and Sprout was kicking even more since they'd been home. Maybe she was reacting to her stress. Margie had driven the girls to school and went back home. She'd reminded Chloe that all she had to do was call if she wanted her to come over, and she was beyond thankful she had her mother close.

Exhausted, and not sleeping well was making her cranky and a nap sounded heavenly. She'd just settled on the couch when her cell phone rang. But when she saw the name she was thrilled.

"Lily. How are you? How's Alex? Is he okay?"

"Hey, I'm okay and yes, Alex is doing better I think." Chloe called bull shit. If Lily's weak voice was any indication, her friend was exhausted, and probably at the end of her rope. How she wished she could be there with her.

"Did he have the second surgery?"

"Yeah. But they still couldn't get all the crap out. The area is too swollen. They're worried they could permanently paralyze him if they try to get the rest of the shit. He's still in the ICU. I have the feeling there's more going on, but they won't tell me anything else."

"Oh no. Have you been able to talk to Alex?"

"Only for a few minutes. He was going into surgery right after we got here, and he was barely coherent afterward. I don't think he even realized I was there. But he's mostly been sleeping. I guess between the anesthesia and the pain meds, he's wiped out."

"Probably for the best. Have you gotten any sleep?"

"No. Not yet. It's been chaotic since we got here. And I wanted to call you first. Right after we landed we got some bad news too."

Chloe dreaded the next words Lily was going to speak.

"Ben didn't make it. He didn't survive the flight from Afghanistan."

"Oh my God. How is Karen?"

"Fucking devastated. Inconsolable. If our flight had taken off an hour later, she wouldn't have had to come." Lily was trying to explain but all Chloe could hear were the deep wrenching sobs. Her heart twisted in sympathy for Karen. She'd been so excited when she found out she was pregnant with their baby. It was their first, and now Ben would never get to meet the little one, and the baby would never know his father.

Chloe couldn't even imagine how she was coping. The horror of finding out he was wounded, then the worry throughout the flight only to land and find out he was gone. That she'd never see him again. Never hug him, kiss him, feel his arms around her. That he'd never hold their child. Tears slid down Chloe's face as she grieved for all those killed or wounded in the attack. Too many.

"Oh my God, Chloe. It could have been Alex. How the fuck would I have dealt with that?"

"But it wasn't. You need to take a deep breath. He's going to be okay. Right?" Chloe needed to take her own advice. To pull herself together to be strong for Lily and Karen and the others when they returned. And for her daughters. It wouldn't be good for them to see her like this.

"I think so. I hope so, but I just don't know."

"You need to think positive, he made it through the surgery, he's in good hands. Hold onto that. If you have to, put it on hold and help Karen while she's there. She'll need someone to lean on."

"True. She's not doing well, they're worried about the baby." Chloe was too, that kind of shock and stress, she couldn't even imagine. "They're flying her back with Ben's body."

"What about Tyler and Mark? Are they well enough to fly back?"

"I don't know. They're in the burn unit. I'm not sure how bad they are. It's been a huge clusterfuck."

"It sounds like it. I wish I was there with you."

"I wish you were too. But you're right, I have to put on my big girl panties. It's going to be a long road. They did tell me that."

"That's okay. Long roads can be navigated."

"Alex won't be coming back to Florida for a while, either. They're sending him to Walter Reed as soon as he's well enough to be transported."

"I'm sure they have specialists there."

"That's what they said. But now I'm not sure when I'll be back either. I could stay at this housing place they have for families."

"Perfect. Now you don't have to worry about him being up there by himself and what you'd do."

"Exactly. I just…"

"I know, Honey. It'll be okay. Yes, I keep saying that, but we have to believe it. Maybe once you get back, Mom can stay with the girls and I'll come up for a couple of days."

"That would be wonderful." Even over the phone, she heard the relief in Lily's voice. Having a friend to lean on was priceless.

"Go rest, Honey. Call me when you wake up if you want to talk. You sound exhausted."

"I am. Sleep sounds amazing. I'm just not sure it'll happen."

"Try. Or maybe someone can give you a sleeping pill. We'll talk later. Love you."

"Love you too."

EPILOGUE

Five months later…

The contractions started at two a.m. Was there some kind of code among babies that they had to wake their parents up in the middle of the night even before they were born? Did any baby arrive during the day? None of hers had, so she shouldn't have been surprised when she was woken out of a sound sleep. Her water was kind enough to wait until she called her mom to let her know it was time—two weeks late.

After mopping up the mess, she grabbed a quick shower and felt better until the next contraction. Holy Crap. Doubled-over and holding her stomach, she almost passed out. Then the cramping started in her back. Her mom better show up soon or this might turn into a home birth.

When Bella was born, she'd called Lily and her mom, and they'd left for the hospital as soon as her mom arrived to watch Lexie. But Lily was still in Washington, D.C. with Alex at Walter Reed. It had been touch and go with Alex for a couple of months, but he'd finally turned the corner and would even be coming home soon. It had been a long battle, a lot longer than any of them had anticipated. Lily had pulled it together after the initial shock and attacked the 'problem' like everything else—with snark and action. She'd have loved to have been in the room the first time she told Alex to get over himself and stop being a pussy. Classic Lily, for sure. Of course, Alex didn't realize that after she'd left his room, she'd called Chloe every day and cried, but it's not like he ever needed to know either.

Logan had another three months left of his deployment. This was definitely the hardest one they'd been through. It was worse for Logan without Alex there too. She'd sent him a text yesterday after her appointment to let him know the doctor said he planned on inducing her if she didn't go into labor by the end of the week. She was already late. But that wasn't going to be necessary, nope. Doubled over, she tried to control the pain with breathing. "Sprout, are you always going to do things on your own terms?" Not that she was sorry, she hated being induced. The fewer meds, the better, because she sure as shit wasn't going to give up the pain meds. Screw that. She was brave but not a masochist. Another contraction wracked her body. Ugh. C'mon mom.

"You need to wait until we get to the hospital, okay? You don't want to freak your sisters out. Trust me." Once the next contraction ended, she went to wake the girls.

Their small bodies were just lumps in their beds, but it made her smile. They were growing so fast and couldn't wait for their baby brother or sister to come home so they could play together. Every day Bella would ask if it was time yet, and every day Chloe would answer the same thing. Not yet.

A gentle shake and a kiss usually did the trick, but it wasn't usually in the middle of the night. But their sibling was coming and didn't care they were all missing beauty sleep. "Time to wake up, Lexie."

"What's wrong, Mommy? It's still dark." Lexie rubbed her eyes and sat up in bed. The hallway light was bright enough to see her wide yawn. She smiled, but the sudden sharp pain in her lower back forced her to sit on the edge of the bed.

"It's time for the baby to come. Grandma's on her way and we need to be ready to go to the hospital as soon as she gets here." Her words pushed Bella's 'on button' and she swore the kid went from zero to sixty in seconds. Jumping out of her bed, she got dressed in the clothes she'd put out for them to wear to school. It would have been funny to watch if the contractions weren't coming faster and making her nauseated.

"The baby has bad timing," Lexie grumbled as she got out of bed and got dressed. Chloe laughed that time. Lexie didn't remember what a newborn baby was like, she'd only been two when Bella was born. There would be a lot of changes over the next few months. But they'd make it work.

By the time Margie arrived, they were waiting in the living room. Chloe had her "go bag" and the girls each clutched the stuffed turtles she'd brought back from Sanibel Island. They'd become their stuffy of choice since then. Did she know her girls or what?

"Are we ready for the new baby?" Margie asked as she walked into the living room.

"What do you think?" Chloe answered as she doubled over.

"Oh dear, you are close, aren't you?"

Nodding, afraid what she'd say if she actually opened her mouth, she grabbed her bag and led the girls outside to her mom's car.

"You do remember the way to the hospital, Mom, don't you?"

"Don't patronize me, young lady, I may be old, but I'm not clueless." The girls giggled in the backseat and Chloe gritted her teeth as another contraction hit. She loved teasing her mother when she had the opportunity, which wasn't often, she was always on top of her game even at almost seventy years old.

In classic movie fashion, Margie pulled the car up to the Emergency Entrance of Willow Haven General Hospital. "Okay, out with you. I'll park, and we'll find you."

Chloe was in no mood to argue and grabbed her bag. She hobbled inside as she clutched her stomach. "When you finally decided you were ready, you weren't fooling around, were you, Sprout?" Chloe mumbled mostly to herself as she went through the sliding glass doors. The ER was almost empty. It's the only good thing about going into labor in the middle of the night. The nurse at intake took one look at her and grabbed a wheelchair.

"How far apart?"

"About two and a half minutes, but it's my third baby."

"Playing the odds huh? Or were you trying to have the baby in the car and make the morning news?" The nurse smiled to soften her words. Chloe knew the tactic was meant to distract the patient from the pain. God bless a good nurse.

"Not really, just waiting on my chariot to arrive," Chloe said then clenched her teeth as she fought back the pain. "Dr. Cohen is my OB/GYN. He had a room reserved for me on Friday. He thought he'd have to induce. Surprise."

"Great. Let's get you checked into L&D. I don't think you have long."

"It better be long enough to get an epidural." The nurse shrugged but didn't say a word, she probably afraid to let her know it was already too late. Chloe figured that with contractions two minutes or less apart it wouldn't be long before she was holding Sprout in her arms.

"Who's with you?"

"My mom and two daughters."

"How old are they?"

"Five and Seven, and just about seventy."

"A sense of humor, huh? You're going to need it. But I'm afraid they won't let the girls in the delivery room."

"I knew that. They'll be waiting for me in the waiting room with my mother."

By the time they'd arrived on the Labor and Delivery floor, she'd had three more contractions and wondered if the baby would come while she was still sitting in the wheelchair. After being transferred into the care of an L&D nurse named Sharon, she was settled in a bed and hooked up to monitors while she waited for Dr. Cohen. At this point, she wasn't sure he'd make it in time.

"It won't be long now. We called Dr. Cohen. He's on his way, but I'm not sure he'll make it from the looks of things."

"I was worried about that."

"It's okay, Dr. Sherman is on call tonight, and he's excellent."

"Did you say Sherman?"

"Yes, do you know him?"

"No." She looked up at the ceiling as the next contraction ripped through her body. Divine intervention? God, are you trying to tell me something? For a moment she contemplated trying to call Logan. Then he'd at least be on the phone when his baby was born.

"Do you have a labor partner with you?"

"Not this time," she answered through gritted teeth.

"No problem, I'll be with you then."

Chloe squeezed her eyes shut as the pain took her breath away.

"Yes, she does. Hi, Princess." The voice cut through her pain-addled brain and her eyes popped open.

"Logan?" She wasn't sure if the pain was producing hallucinations or her handsome husband was really standing next to her. When he took her hand, she squeezed it as hard as she could. When he winced, she knew it wasn't her imagination.

"Shit, woman. Have you been spinach loading? Maybe I should call you Popeye."

Wonderful, funny, Logan. How he'd gotten there she didn't care, but he was there, and for the first time he'd get to see his child being born.

"Oh God."

He must have looked at the nurse because she chuckled. "I guess you haven't been through this before?"

"No, unfortunately."

"It's going to get worse before it gets better. But you'll have a great present at the end. And it will keep giving—or rather taking—for the next twenty years or so."

Chloe already loved Sharon, she was her type of nurse. Funny, no-nonsense and would make sure everything went like clockwork. "You need to change out of those fatigues, soldier. Come with me."

"I'll be right back, Princess. Don't go anywhere."

As if! Geesh. If she could have, she would have punched him. Actually, no she wouldn't. The only thing that could make her happier was to already be holding her baby in her arms. The pain needed to be done.

Once Logan returned in his scrubs, they wheeled her into the delivery room. The bright lights blinded her. Another contraction hit, and this time Logan held her hand through it. Somehow that made it better.

"Hi, Mrs. Mitchell. I'm Dr. Sherman, and I'll be playing the role of catcher this evening." It took her a moment to realize what he meant, and she rolled her eyes as she breathed through a contraction. He was lucky she didn't tell him to take a flying whatever at a rolling donut. You don't mess with women in labor and live to tell about it.

"Doc, your name is Sherman?"

"Yes, it is. I know I'm not your wife's regular doctor but he's not going to make it. She's already fully dilated, and the baby's head is crowning."

"What should I do?"

"Just keep doing what you are. She's too close for pain meds and this may be a bit uncomfortable."

What was it with doctors and the word uncomfortable? Seriously? Try taking your bottom lip and stapling it to your forehead, that's about what it felt like. Thankfully, Sprout seemed determined to take the express route. Fifteen minutes later in a blur of pain and happiness, Dr. Sherman announced that they were the parents of a little baby boy.

"So, what's this little one's name?" Sharon asked as she placed the baby in Chloe's arms.

"Andrew Sherman Mitchell." Logan's gaze slid from his new son to her eyes. "I think it works, don't you?"

"Yes. It's a perfect name for our little man," he said as he reverently touched his son's face.

A short time later her mom and the girls came in to meet little Andy. She didn't know if the girls were more excited to see Logan or the new baby, but in the end, the baby won.

"How long are you able to stay?"

"Forever, Princess. I'm home for good," he whispered against her lips in a kiss full of love and the promise of new beginnings.

The End

If you enjoyed this book, the best way to let the author know is through a review. It's easy and only takes a few words but will go a long way to help spread the word and make the author's day! Thank you, Lynne xoxo

If you loved *A Soldier's Forever*, you'll really love *A Soldier's Triumph*, Alex and Lily's story. Here's a sneak preview.

∽

They'd been home a week, and Lily was already pulling her hair out. Alex had a long road ahead of him if she didn't kill him first. What they'd gone through at Walter Reed was tough, but this was a thousand times worse. In the hospital, there'd been a buffer between her and his pain and moodiness. The doctors, volunteers, nurses, and therapists had been in and out of his hospital room. Now it was all on her and she was worried she couldn't be the woman, the support, the wall, he needed her to be.

Sheer terror and worry about losing him had morphed into the overwhelming joy that he'd survive and that she wouldn't lose the man of her dreams. Since they'd met, somehow, she'd known he was her destiny. Not one to believe in love at first sight, she fought it, but eventually, they both gave in after they got past the friends to lovers' phase. And she'd never looked back.

The reality of his recovery and the agony he faced daily shredded her heart and scared the ever-living shit out of her. If it hadn't been for her best friend, Chloe, she'd have lost it long before now. Even with a new baby and her young daughters, Lexie and Bella, she'd taken every one of Lily's calls. Listened to her as she sobbed her heart out for countless hours after leaving Walter Reed National Military Hospital every evening.

ABOUT THE AUTHOR

Lynne St. James is the author of over seventeen books in paranormal, new adult, and contemporary romance. She lives in the mostly sunny state of Florida with her husband, an eighty-five-pound fluffy Dalmatian-mutt horse-dog, a small Yorkie-poo, and a cat named Pumpkin who rules them all.

When Lynne's not writing stories about second chances and conquering adversity with happily-ever-afters, you'll find her with a mug of coffee, a crochet hook, or a book (or e-reader) in her hand.

Where to find Lynne:
Email: lynne@lynnestjames.com
Website: http://lynnestjames.com
VIP Newsletter sign-up: http://eepurl.com/bT99Fj

- facebook.com/authorLynneStJames
- twitter.com/lynnestjames
- instagram.com/lynnestjames
- amazon.com/Lynne-St.James
- bookbub.com/profile/lynne-st-james

BOOKS BY LYNNE ST. JAMES

Beyond Valor Series

A Soldier's Gift, Book 1

A Soldier's Forever (*Previously A Soldier's Surprise*), Book 2

A Soldier's Triumph, Book 3 – ESP Agency Novel

A Soldier's Protection (Previously Protecting Faith), Book 4 – (re-release soon)

A Soldier's Pledge, Book 5 – ESP Agency Novel

A Soldier's Destiny (Previously Guarding Aurora), Book 6 – (re-release soon)

A Soldier's Temptation (Previously Protecting Ariana), Book 7 – (re-release soon)

A Soldier's Homecoming, Book 8 – ESP Agency Novel (coming soon)

A Soldier's Redemption, Book 9 – ESP Agency Novel (coming Soon)

Raining Chaos Series

Taming Chaos, Book 1

Seducing Wrath, Book 2

Music under the Mistletoe, Book 2.5 – A Raining Chaos Christmas (Novella)

Tempting Flame, Book 3

Anamchara Series

Embracing Her Desires, Book 1

Embracing Her Surrender, Book 2

Embracing Her Love, Book 3

The Vampires of Eternity Series

Twice Bitten Not Shy, Book 1

Twice Bitten to Paradise, Book 2

Twice Bitten and Bewitched, Book 3